THE SCHOOL FO]

A COMEDY
A PORTRAIT

Philippa Bradley.

Richard Brinsley Sheridan

- Social background / Context.
- Awareness of fashion and Frances Abington.
- Fashionability and Sir Peter.
- Lady Teazle's independence.

Table of Contents

THE TEXT OF THE SCHOOL FOR SCANDAL

The text of THE SCHOOL FOR SCANDAL in this edition is taken, by Mr. Fraser Rae's generous permission, from his SHERIDAN'S PLAYS NOW PRINTED AS HE WROTE THEM. In his Prefatory Notes (xxxvii), Mr. Rae writes: "The manuscript of it [THE SCHOOL FOR SCANDAL] in Sheridan's own handwriting is preserved at Frampton Court and is now printed in this volume. This version differs in many respects from that which is generally known, and I think it is even better than that which has hitherto been read and acted. As I have endeavoured to reproduce the works of Sheridan as he wrote them, I may be told that he was a bad hand at punctuating and very bad at spelling. . . . But Sheridan's shortcomings as a speller have been exaggerated." Lest "Sheridan's shortcomings" either in spelling or in punctuation should obscure the text, I have, in this edition, inserted in brackets some explanatory suggestions. It has seemed best, also, to adopt a uniform method for indicating stage-directions and abbreviations of the names of characters. There can be no gain to the reader in reproducing, for example, Sheridan's different indications for the part of Lady Sneerwell---LADY SNEERWELL, LADY SNEER., LADY SN., and LADY S.---or his varying use of EXIT and EX., or his inconsistencies in the use of italics in the stage-directions. Since, however, Sheridan's biographers, from Moore to Fraser Rae, have shown that no authorised or correct edition of THE SCHOOL FOR SCANDAL was published in Sheridan's lifetime, there seems unusual justification for reproducing the text of the play itself with absolute fidelity to the original manuscript. Mr. Ridgway, who repeatedly sought to obtain a copy corrected by the author, according to Moore's account (LIFE OF SHERIDAN, I. p. 260), "was told by Mr. Sheridan, as an excuse for keeping it back, that he had been nineteen years endeavouring to satisfy himself with the style of The School for Scandal, but had not yet succeeded." Mr. Rae (SHERIDAN, I. p. 332) recorded his discovery of the manuscript of "two acts of The School for Scandal prepared by Sheridan for publication," and hoped, before his death, to publish this partial revision. Numberless unauthorized changes in the play have been made for histrionic purposes, from the first undated Dublin edition to that of Mr. Augustin Daly. Current texts may usually be traced, directly or indirectly, to the two-volume Murray edition of Sheridan's plays, in 1821. Some of the changes from the original manuscript, such as the blending of the parts of Miss Verjuice and Snake, are doubtless effective for reasons of dramatic economy, but many of the "cuts" are to be regretted from the reader's standpoint. The student of English drama will prefer Sheridan's own text to editorial emendations, however clever or effective for dramatic ends.

THE SCHOOL FOR SCANDAL

ADDRESSED TO MRS. CREWE,
WITH THE COMEDY OF THE SCHOOL FOR SCANDAL

Tell me, ye prim adepts in Scandal's school,
    Who rail by precept, and detract by rule,
    Lives there no character, so tried, so known,
    So deck'd with grace, and so unlike your own,
    That even you assist her fame to raise,
    Approve by envy, and by silence praise!---
    Attend!---a model shall attract your view---
    Daughters of calumny, I summon you!
    You shall decide if this a portrait prove,
    Or fond creation of the Muse and Love.---
    Attend, ye virgin critics, shrewd and sage,
    Ye matron censors of this childish age,
    Whose peering eye and wrinkled front declare
    A fixt antipathy to young and fair;
    By cunning, cautious; or by nature, cold,
    In maiden madness, virulently bold!---
    Attend! ye skilled to coin the precious tale,
    Creating proof, where innuendos fail!
    Whose practised memories, cruelly exact,
    Omit no circumstance, except the fact!---
    Attend, all ye who boast,---or old or young,---
    The living libel of a slanderous tongue!
    So shall my theme as far contrasted be,
    As saints by fiends, or hymns by calumny.
    Come, gentle Amoret (for 'neath that name,
    In worthier verse is sung thy beauty's fame);
    Come---for but thee who seeks the Muse? and while
    Celestial blushes check thy conscious smile,
    With timid grace, and hesitating eye,
    The perfect model, which I boast, supply:---
    Vain Muse! couldst thou the humblest sketch create
    Of her, or slightest charm couldst imitate---
    Could thy blest strain in kindred colours trace
    The faintest wonder of her form and face---
    Poets would study the immortal line,
    And REYNOLDS own HIS art subdued by thine;
    That art, which well might added lustre give
    To Nature's best and Heaven's superlative:
    On GRANBY'S cheek might bid new glories rise,
    Or point a purer beam from DEVON'S eyes!
    Hard is the task to shape that beauty's praise,
    Whose judgment scorns the homage flattery pays!
    But praising Amoret we cannot err,
    No tongue o'ervalues Heaven, or flatters her!

Yet she, by Fate's perverseness---she alone
Would doubt our truth, nor deem such praise her own!
Adorning Fashion, unadorn'd by dress,
Simple from taste, and not from carelessness;
Discreet in gesture, in deportment mild,
Not stiff with prudence, nor uncouthly wild:
No state has AMORET! no studied mien;
She frowns no GODDESS, and she moves no QUEEN.
The softer charm that in her manner lies
Is framed to captivate, yet not surprise;
It justly suits th' expression of her face,---
'Tis less than dignity, and more than grace!
On her pure cheek the native hue is such,
That, form'd by Heav'n to be admired so much,
The hand divine, with a less partial care,
Might well have fix'd a fainter crimson there,
And bade the gentle inmate of her breast,---
Inshrined Modesty!---supply the rest.
But who the peril of her lips shall paint?
Strip them of smiles---still, still all words are faint!
But moving Love himself appears to teach
Their action, though denied to rule her speech;
And thou who seest her speak and dost not hear,
Mourn not her distant accents 'scape thine ear;
Viewing those lips, thou still may'st make pretence
To judge of what she says, and swear 'tis sense:
Cloth'd with such grace, with such expression fraught,
They move in meaning, and they pause in thought!
But dost thou farther watch, with charm'd surprise,
The mild irresolution of her eyes,
Curious to mark how frequent they repose,
In brief eclipse and momentary close---
Ah! seest thou not an ambush'd Cupid there,
Too tim'rous of his charge, with jealous care
Veils and unveils those beams of heav'nly light,
Too full, too fatal else, for mortal sight?
Nor yet, such pleasing vengeance fond to meet,
In pard'ning dimples hope a safe retreat.
What though her peaceful breast should ne'er allow
Subduing frowns to arm her altered brow,
By Love, I swear, and by his gentle wiles,
More fatal still the mercy of her smiles!
Thus lovely, thus adorn'd, possessing all
Of bright or fair that can to woman fall,
The height of vanity might well be thought
Prerogative in her, and Nature's fault.
Yet gentle AMORET, in mind supreme
As well as charms, rejects the vainer theme;
And, half mistrustful of her beauty's store,
She barbs with wit those darts too keen before:---

Read in all knowledge that her sex should reach,
Though GREVILLE, or the MUSE, should deign to teach,
Fond to improve, nor tim'rous to discern
How far it is a woman's grace to learn;
In MILLAR'S dialect she would not prove
Apollo's priestess, but Apollo's love,
Graced by those signs which truth delights to own,
The timid blush, and mild submitted tone:
Whate'er she says, though sense appear throughout,
Displays the tender hue of female doubt;
Deck'd with that charm, how lovely wit appears,
How graceful SCIENCE, when that robe she wears!
Such too her talents, and her bent of mind,
As speak a sprightly heart by thought refined:
A taste for mirth, by contemplation school'd,
A turn for ridicule, by candour ruled,
A scorn of folly, which she tries to hide;
An awe of talent, which she owns with pride!
   Peace, idle Muse! no more thy strain prolong,
But yield a theme thy warmest praises wrong;
Just to her merit, though thou canst not raise
Thy feeble verse, behold th' acknowledged praise
Has spread conviction through the envious train,
And cast a fatal gloom o'er Scandal's reign!
And lo! each pallid hag, with blister'd tongue,
Mutters assent to all thy zeal has sung---
Owns all the colours just---the outline true;
Thee my inspirer, and my MODEL---CREWE!

DRAMATIS PERSONAE2

SIR PETER TEAZLE	Mr. King
SIR OLIVER SURFACE	Mr. Yates
YOUNG SURFACE	Mr. Palmer
CHARLES (his Brother)	Mr. Smith
CRABTREE	Mr. Parsons
SIR BENJAMIN BACKBITE	Mr. Dodd
ROWLEY	Mr. Aikin
SPUNGE	
MOSES	
SNAKE	
CARELESS---and other companions to CHARLES	

LADY TEAZLE
MARIA
LADY SNEERWELL
MRS. CANDOUR
MISS VERJUICE

PROLOGUE WRITTEN BY MR. GARRICK

A school for Scandal! tell me, I beseech you,
    Needs there a school this modish art to teach you?
    No need of lessons now, the knowing think;
    We might as well be taught to eat and drink.
    Caused by a dearth of scandal, should the vapours
    Distress our fair ones---let them read the papers;
    Their powerful mixtures such disorders hit;
    Crave what you will---there's quantum sufficit.
    "Lord!" cries my Lady Wormwood (who loves tattle,
    And puts much salt and pepper in her prattle),
    Just risen at noon, all night at cards when threshing
    Strong tea and scandal---"Bless me, how refreshing!
    Give me the papers, Lisp---how bold and free! [Sips.]
    LAST NIGHT LORD L. [Sips] WAS CAUGHT WITH LADY D.
    For aching heads what charming sal volatile! [Sips.]
    IF MRS. B. WILL STILL CONTINUE FLIRTING,
    WE HOPE SHE'LL draw, OR WE'LL undraw THE CURTAIN.
    Fine satire, poz---in public all abuse it,
    But, by ourselves [Sips], our praise we can't refuse it.
    Now, Lisp, read you---there, at that dash and star:"
    "Yes, ma'am---A CERTAIN LORD HAD BEST BEWARE,
    WHO LIVES NOT TWENTY MILES FROM GROSVENOR SQUARE;
    FOR, SHOULD HE LADY W. FIND WILLING,
    WORMWOOD IS BITTER"------"Oh! that's me! the villain!
    Throw it behind the fire, and never more
    Let that vile paper come within my door."
    Thus at our friends we laugh, who feel the dart;
    To reach our feelings, we ourselves must smart.
    Is our young bard so young, to think that he
    Can stop the full spring-tide of calumny?
    Knows he the world so little, and its trade?
    Alas! the devil's sooner raised than laid.
    So strong, so swift, the monster there's no gagging:
    Cut Scandal's head off, still the tongue is wagging.
    Proud of your smiles once lavishly bestow'd,
    Again our young Don Quixote takes the road;
    To show his gratitude he draws his pen,
    And seeks his hydra, Scandal, in his den.
    For your applause all perils he would through---
    He'll fight---that's write---a cavalliero true,
    Till every drop of blood---that's ink---is spilt for you.

ACT I

SCENE I.---LADY SNEERWELL'S House

LADY SNEERWELL at her dressing table with LAPPET; MISS VERJUICE drinking chocolate

LADY SNEERWELL. The Paragraphs you say were all inserted:

VERJUICE. They were Madam---and as I copied them myself in a feigned Hand there can be no suspicion whence they came.

LADY SNEERWELL. Did you circulate the Report of Lady Brittle's Intrigue with Captain Boastall?

VERJUICE. Madam by this Time Lady Brittle is the Talk of half the Town---and I doubt not in a week the Men will toast her as a Demirep.

LADY SNEERWELL. What have you done as to the insinuation as to a certain Baronet's Lady and a certain Cook.

VERJUICE. That is in as fine a Train as your Ladyship could wish. I told the story yesterday to my own maid with directions to communicate it directly to my Hairdresser. He I am informed has a Brother who courts a Milliners' Prentice in Pallmall whose mistress has a first cousin whose sister is Feme [Femme] de Chambre to Mrs. Clackit---so that in the common course of Things it must reach Mrs. Clackit's Ears within four-and-twenty hours and then you know the Business is as good as done.

LADY SNEERWELL. Why truly Mrs. Clackit has a very pretty Talent---a great deal of industry---yet---yes---been tolerably successful in her way---To my knowledge she has been the cause of breaking off six matches[,] of three sons being disinherited and four Daughters being turned out of Doors. Of three several Elopements, as many close confinements---nine separate maintenances and two Divorces.---nay I have more than once traced her causing a Tete-a-Tete in the Town and Country Magazine---when the Parties perhaps had never seen each other's Faces before in the course of their Lives.

VERJUICE. She certainly has Talents.

LADY SNEERWELL. But her manner is gross.

VERJUICE. 'Tis very true. She generally designs well[,] has a free tongue and a bold invention---but her colouring is too dark and her outline often extravagant---She wants that delicacy of Tint---and mellowness of sneer---which distinguish your Ladyship's Scandal.

LADY SNEERWELL. Ah you are Partial Verjuice.

VERJUICE. Not in the least---everybody allows that Lady Sneerwell can do more with a word or a Look than many can with the most laboured Detail even when they happen to have a little truth on their side to support it.

LADY SNEERWELL. Yes my dear Verjuice. I am no Hypocrite to deny the satisfaction I reap from the Success of my Efforts. Wounded myself, in the early part of my Life by the envenomed Tongue of Slander I confess I have since known no Pleasure equal to the reducing others to the Level of my own injured Reputation.

VERJUICE. Nothing can be more natural---But my dear Lady Sneerwell There is one affair in which you have lately employed me, wherein, I confess I am at a Loss to guess your motives.

LADY SNEERWELL. I conceive you mean with respect to my neighbour, Sir Peter Teazle, and his Family---Lappet.---And has my conduct in this matter really appeared to you so mysterious?

[Exit MAID.]

9

VERJUICE. Entirely so.

LADY SNEERWELL. [VERJUICE.?] An old Batchelor as Sir Peter was[,] having taken a young wife from out of the Country---as Lady Teazle is---are certainly fair subjects for a little mischievous raillery---but here are two young men---to whom Sir Peter has acted as a kind of Guardian since their Father's death, the eldest possessing the most amiable Character and universally well spoken of[,] the youngest the most dissipated and extravagant young Fellow in the Kingdom, without Friends or caracter---the former one an avowed admirer of yours and apparently your Favourite[,] the latter attached to Maria Sir Peter's ward---and confessedly beloved by her. Now on the face of these circumstances it is utterly unaccountable to me why you a young Widow with no great jointure---should not close with the passion of a man of such character and expectations as Mr. Surface---and more so why you should be so uncommonly earnest to destroy the mutual Attachment subsisting between his Brother Charles and Maria.

LADY SNEERWELL. Then at once to unravel this mistery---I must inform you that Love has no share whatever in the intercourse between Mr. Surface and me.

VERJUICE. No!

LADY SNEERWELL. His real attachment is to Maria or her Fortune---but finding in his Brother a favoured Rival, He has been obliged to mask his Pretensions---and profit by my Assistance.

VERJUICE. Yet still I am more puzzled why you should interest yourself in his success.

LADY SNEERWELL. Heavens! how dull you are! cannot you surmise the weakness which I hitherto, thro' shame have concealed even from you---must I confess that Charles---that Libertine, that extravagant, that Bankrupt in Fortune and Reputation---that He it is for whom I am thus anxious and malicious and to gain whom I would sacrifice---everything------

VERJUICE. Now indeed---your conduct appears consistent and I no longer wonder at your enmity to Maria, but how came you and Surface so confidential?

LADY SNEERWELL. For our mutual interest---but I have found out him a long time since[,] altho' He has contrived to deceive everybody beside---I know him to be artful selfish and malicious---while with Sir Peter, and indeed with all his acquaintance, He passes for a youthful Miracle of Prudence---good sense and Benevolence.

VERJUICE. Yes yes---I know Sir Peter vows He has not his equal in England; and, above all, He praises him as a MAN OF SENTIMENT.

LADY SNEERWELL. True and with the assistance of his sentiments and hypocrisy he has brought Sir Peter entirely in his interests with respect to Maria and is now I believe attempting to flatter Lady Teazle into the same good opinion towards him---while poor Charles has no Friend in the House---though I fear he has a powerful one in Maria's Heart, against whom we must direct our schemes.

SERVANT. Mr. Surface.

LADY SNEERWELL. Shew him up. He generally calls about this Time. I don't wonder at People's giving him to me for a Lover.

Enter SURFACE

SURFACE. My dear Lady Sneerwell, how do you do to-day---your most obedient.

LADY SNEERWELL. Miss Verjuice has just been arraigning me on our mutual attachment now; but I have informed her of our real views and the Purposes for which our Geniuses at present co-operate. You know how useful she has been to us---and believe me the confidence is not ill-placed.

SURFACE. Madam, it is impossible for me to suspect that a Lady of Miss Verjuice's sensibility and discernment------

LADY SNEERWELL. Well---well---no compliments now---but tell me when you saw your mistress or what is more material to me your Brother.

SURFACE. I have not seen either since I saw you---but I can inform you that they are at present at Variance---some of your stories have taken good effect on Maria.

LADY SNEERWELL. Ah! my dear Verjuice the merit of this belongs to you. But do your Brother's Distresses encrease?

SURFACE. Every hour. I am told He had another execution in his house yesterday---in short his Dissipation and extravagance exceed anything I have ever heard of.

LADY SNEERWELL. Poor Charles!

SURFACE. True Madam---notwithstanding his Vices one can't help feeling for him---ah poor Charles! I'm sure I wish it was in my Power to be of any essential Service to him---for the man who does not share in the Distresses of a Brother---even though merited by his own misconduct---deserves------

LADY SNEERWELL. O Lud you are going to be moral, and forget that you are among Friends.

SURFACE. Egad, that's true---I'll keep that sentiment till I see Sir Peter. However it is certainly a charity to rescue Maria from such a Libertine who---if He is to be reclaim'd, can be so only by a Person of your Ladyship's superior accomplishments and understanding.

VERJUICE. 'Twould be a Hazardous experiment.

SURFACE. But---Madam---let me caution you to place no more confidence in our Friend Snake the Libeller---I have lately detected him in frequent conference with old Rowland [Rowley] who was formerly my Father's Steward and has never been a friend of mine.

LADY SNEERWELL. I'm not disappointed in Snake, I never suspected the fellow to have virtue enough to be faithful even to his own Villany.

Enter MARIA

Maria my dear---how do you do---what's the matter?

MARIA. O here is that disagreeable lover of mine, Sir Benjamin Backbite, has just call'd at my guardian's with his odious Uncle Crabtree---so I slipt out and ran hither to avoid them.

LADY SNEERWELL. Is that all?

VERJUICE. Lady Sneerwell---I'll go and write the Letter I mention'd to you.

SURFACE. If my Brother Charles had been of the Party, madam, perhaps you would not have been so much alarmed.

LADY SNEERWELL. Nay now---you are severe for I dare swear the Truth of the matter is Maria heard YOU were here---but my dear---what has Sir Benjamin done that you should avoid him so------

MARIA. Oh He has done nothing---but his conversation is a perpetual Libel on all his Acquaintance.

SURFACE. Aye and the worst of it is there is no advantage in not knowing Them, for He'll abuse a stranger just as soon as his best Friend---and Crabtree is as bad.

LADY SNEERWELL. Nay but we should make allowance[---]Sir Benjamin is a wit and a poet.

MARIA. For my Part---I own madam---wit loses its respect with me, when I see it in company with malice.---What do you think, Mr. Surface?

SURFACE. Certainly, Madam, to smile at the jest which plants a Thorn on another's Breast is to become a principal in the mischief.

LADY SNEERWELL. Pshaw---there's no possibility of being witty without a little [ill] nature---

the malice of a good thing is the Barb that makes it stick.---What's your opinion, Mr. Surface?

SURFACE. Certainly madam---that conversation where the Spirit of Raillery is suppressed will ever appear tedious and insipid---

MARIA. Well I'll not debate how far Scandal may be allowable---but in a man I am sure it is always contemtable.---We have Pride, envy, Rivalship, and a Thousand motives to depreciate each other---but the male-slanderer must have the cowardice of a woman before He can traduce one.

LADY SNEERWELL. I wish my Cousin Verjuice hadn't left us---she should embrace you.

SURFACE. Ah! she's an old maid and is privileged of course.

Enter SERVANT

Madam Mrs. Candour is below and if your Ladyship's at leisure will leave her carriage.

LADY SNEERWELL. Beg her to walk in. Now, Maria[,] however here is a Character to your Taste, for tho' Mrs. Candour is a little talkative everybody allows her to be the best-natured and best sort of woman.

MARIA. Yes with a very gross affectation of good Nature and Benevolence---she does more mischief than the Direct malice of old Crabtree.

SURFACE. Efaith 'tis very true Lady Sneerwell---Whenever I hear the current running again the characters of my Friends, I never think them in such Danger as when Candour undertakes their Defence.

LADY SNEERWELL. Hush here she is------

Enter MRS. CANDOUR

MRS. CANDOUR. My dear Lady Sneerwell how have you been this Century. I have never seen you tho' I have heard of you very often.---Mr. Surface---the World says scandalous things of you---but indeed it is no matter what the world says, for I think one hears nothing else but scandal.

SURFACE. Just so, indeed, Ma'am.

MRS. CANDOUR. Ah Maria Child---what[!] is the whole affair off between you and Charles? His extravagance; I presume---The Town talks of nothing else------

MARIA. I am very sorry, Ma'am, the Town has so little to do.

MRS. CANDOUR. True, true, Child; but there's no stopping people's Tongues. I own I was hurt to hear it---as I indeed was to learn from the same quarter that your guardian, Sir Peter[,] and Lady Teazle have not agreed lately so well as could be wish'd.

MARIA. 'Tis strangely impertinent for people to busy themselves so.

MRS. CANDOUR. Very true, Child; but what's to be done? People will talk---there's no preventing it.---why it was but yesterday I was told that Miss Gadabout had eloped with Sir Filagree Flirt. But, Lord! there is no minding what one hears; tho' to be sure I had this from very good authority.

MARIA. Such reports are highly scandalous.

MRS. CANDOUR. So they are Child---shameful! shameful! but the world is so censorious no character escapes. Lord, now! who would have suspected your friend, Miss Prim, of an indiscretion Yet such is the ill-nature of people, that they say her unkle stopped her last week just as she was stepping into a Postchaise with her Dancing-master.

MARIA. I'll answer for't there are no grounds for the Report.

MRS. CANDOUR. Oh, no foundation in the world I dare swear[;] no more probably than for the story circulated last month, of Mrs. Festino's affair with Colonel Cassino---tho' to be sure that matter was never rightly clear'd up.

SURFACE. The license of invention some people take is monstrous indeed.

MARIA. 'Tis so but in my opinion, those who report such things are equally culpable.

MRS. CANDOUR. To be sure they are[;] Tale Bearers are as bad as the Tale makers---'tis an old observation and a very true one---but what's to be done as I said before---how will you prevent People from talking---to-day, Mrs. Clackitt assured me, Mr. and Mrs. Honeymoon were at last become mere man and wife---like [the rest of their] acquaintance---she likewise hinted that a certain widow in the next street had got rid of her Dropsy and recovered her shape in a most surprising manner---at the same [time] Miss Tattle, who was by affirm'd, that Lord Boffalo had discover'd his Lady at a house of no extraordinary Fame---and that Sir Harry Bouquet and Tom Saunter were to measure swords on a similar Provocation. But---Lord! do you think I would report these Things---No, no[!] Tale Bearers as I said before are just as bad as the talemakers.

SURFACE. Ah! Mrs. Candour, if everybody had your Forbearance and good nature---

MRS. CANDOUR. I confess Mr. Surface I cannot bear to hear People traduced behind their Backs[;] and when ugly circumstances come out against our acquaintances I own I always love to think the best---by the bye I hope 'tis not true that your Brother is absolutely ruin'd---

SURFACE. I am afraid his circumstances are very bad indeed, Ma'am---

MRS. CANDOUR. Ah! I heard so---but you must tell him to keep up his Spirits---everybody almost is in the same way---Lord Spindle, Sir Thomas Splint, Captain Quinze, and Mr. Nickit---

all up, I hear, within this week; so, if Charles is undone, He'll find half his Acquaintance ruin'd too, and that, you know, is a consolation---

SURFACE. Doubtless, Ma'am---a very great one.

Enter SERVANT

SERVANT. Mr. Crabtree and Sir Benjamin Backbite.

LADY SNEERWELL. Soh! Maria, you see your lover pursues you---Positively you shan't escape.

Enter CRABTREE and SIR BENJAMIN BACKBITE

CRABTREE. Lady Sneerwell, I kiss your hand. Mrs. Candour I don't believe you are acquainted with my Nephew Sir Benjamin Backbite---Egad, Ma'am, He has a pretty wit---and is a pretty Poet too isn't He Lady Sneerwell?

SIR BENJAMIN. O fie, Uncle!

CRABTREE. Nay egad it's true---I back him at a Rebus or a Charade against the best Rhymer in the Kingdom---has your Ladyship heard the Epigram he wrote last week on Lady Frizzle's Feather catching Fire---Do Benjamin repeat it---or the Charade you made last Night extempore at Mrs. Drowzie's conversazione---Come now your first is the Name of a Fish, your second a great naval commander---and

SIR BENJAMIN. Dear Uncle---now---prithee------

CRABTREE. Efaith, Ma'am---'twould surprise you to hear how ready he is at all these Things.

LADY SNEERWELL. I wonder Sir Benjamin you never publish anything.

SIR BENJAMIN. To say truth, Ma'am, 'tis very vulgar to Print and as my little Productions are mostly Satires and Lampoons I find they circulate more by giving copies in confidence to the Friends of the Parties---however I have some love-Elegies, which, when favoured with this lady's smile I mean to give to the Public.

[Pointing to MARIA.]

CRABTREE. 'Fore Heaven, ma'am, they'll immortalize you---you'll be handed down to Posterity, like Petrarch's Laura, or Waller's Sacharissa.

SIR BENJAMIN. Yes Madam I think you will like them---when you shall see in a beautiful

Quarto Page how a neat rivulet of Text shall meander thro' a meadow of margin---'fore Gad, they will be the most elegant Things of their kind---

CRABTREE. But Ladies, have you heard the news?

MRS. CANDOUR. What, Sir, do you mean the Report of------

CRABTREE. No ma'am that's not it.---Miss Nicely is going to be married to her own Footman.

MRS. CANDOUR. Impossible!

CRABTREE. Ask Sir Benjamin.

SIR BENJAMIN. 'Tis very true, Ma'am---everything is fixed and the wedding Livery bespoke.

CRABTREE. Yes and they say there were pressing reasons for't.

MRS. CANDOUR. It cannot be---and I wonder any one should believe such a story of so prudent a Lady as Miss Nicely.

SIR BENJAMIN. O Lud! ma'am, that's the very reason 'twas believed at once. She has always been so cautious and so reserved, that everybody was sure there was some reason for it at bottom.

LADY SNEERWELL. Yes a Tale of Scandal is as fatal to the Reputation of a prudent Lady of her stamp as a Fever is generally to those of the strongest Constitutions, but there is a sort of puny sickly Reputation, that is always ailing yet will outlive the robuster characters of a hundred Prudes.

SIR BENJAMIN. True Madam there are Valetudinarians in Reputation as well as constitution---who being conscious of their weak Part, avoid the least breath of air, and supply their want of Stamina by care and circumspection---

MRS. CANDOUR. Well but this may be all mistake---You know, Sir Benjamin very trifling circumstances often give rise to the most injurious Tales.

CRABTREE. That they do I'll be sworn Ma'am---did you ever hear how Miss Shepherd came to lose her Lover and her Character last summer at Tunbridge---Sir Benjamin you remember it---

SIR BENJAMIN. O to be sure the most whimsical circumstance---

LADY SNEERWELL. How was it Pray---

CRABTREE. Why one evening at Mrs. Ponto's Assembly---the conversation happened to turn on the difficulty of breeding Nova-Scotia Sheep in this country---says a young Lady in company[, "]I have known instances of it[---]for Miss Letitia Shepherd, a first cousin of mine, had a Nova-Scotia Sheep that produced her Twins.["---"]What!["] cries the old Dowager Lady Dundizzy (who you know is as deaf as a Post), ["]has Miss Letitia Shepherd had twins["]---This Mistake---as you may imagine, threw the whole company into a fit of Laughing---However 'twas the next morning everywhere reported and in a few Days believed by the whole Town, that Miss Letitia Shepherd had actually been brought to Bed of a fine Boy and Girl---and in less than a week there were People who could name the Father, and the Farm House where the Babies were put out to Nurse.

LADY SNEERWELL. Strange indeed!

CRABTREE. Matter of Fact, I assure you---O Lud! Mr. Surface pray is it true that your uncle Sir Oliver is coming home---

SURFACE. Not that I know of indeed Sir.

CRABTREE. He has been in the East Indies a long time---you can scarcely remember him---I believe---sad comfort on his arrival to hear how your Brother has gone on!

SURFACE. Charles has been imprudent Sir to be sure[;] but I hope no Busy people have already prejudiced Sir Oliver against him---He may reform---

SIR BENJAMIN. To be sure He may---for my Part I never believed him to be so utterly void of Principle as People say---and tho' he has lost all his Friends I am told nobody is better spoken of---by the Jews.

CRABTREE. That's true egad nephew---if the Old Jewry was a Ward I believe Charles would be an alderman---no man more popular there, 'fore Gad I hear He pays as many annuities as the Irish Tontine and that whenever He's sick they have Prayers for the recovery of his Health in the synagogue---

SIR BENJAMIN. Yet no man lives in greater Splendour:---they tell me when He entertains his Friends---He can sit down to dinner with a dozen of his own Securities, have a score Tradesmen waiting in the Anti-Chamber, and an officer behind every guest's Chair.

SURFACE. This may be entertainment to you Gentlemen but you pay very little regard to the Feelings of a Brother.

MARIA. Their malice is intolerable---Lady Sneerwell I must wish you a good morning---I'm not very well.

[Exit MARIA.]

MRS. CANDOUR. O dear she chang'd colour very much!

LADY SNEERWELL. Do Mrs. Candour follow her---she may want assistance.

MRS. CANDOUR. That I will with all my soul ma'am.---Poor dear Girl---who knows---what her situation may be!

[Exit MRS. CANDOUR.]

LADY SNEERWELL. 'Twas nothing but that she could not bear to hear Charles reflected on notwithstanding their difference.

SIR BENJAMIN. The young Lady's Penchant is obvious.

CRABTREE. But Benjamin---you mustn't give up the Pursuit for that---follow her and put her into good humour---repeat her some of your verses---come, I'll assist you---

SIR BENJAMIN. Mr. Surface I did not mean to hurt you---but depend on't your Brother is utterly undone---

[Going.]

CRABTREE. O Lud! aye---undone---as ever man was---can't raise a guinea.

SIR BENJAMIN. And everything sold---I'm told---that was movable---

[Going.]

CRABTREE. I was at his house---not a thing left but some empty Bottles that were overlooked and the Family Pictures, which I believe are framed in the Wainscot.

[Going.]

SIR BENJAMIN. And I'm very sorry to hear also some bad stories against him.

[Going.]

CRABTREE. O He has done many mean things---that's certain!

SIR BENJAMIN. But however as He is your Brother------

[Going.]

CRABTREE. We'll tell you all another opportunity.

[Exeunt.]

LADY SNEERWELL. Ha! ha! ha! 'tis very hard for them to leave a subject they have not quite run down.

SURFACE. And I believe the Abuse was no more acceptable to your Ladyship than Maria.

LADY SNEERWELL. I doubt her Affections are farther engaged than we imagin'd but the Family are to be here this Evening so you may as well dine where you are and we shall have an opportunity of observing farther---in the meantime, I'll go and plot Mischief and you shall study Sentiments.

[Exeunt.]

SCENE II.---SIR PETER'S House

Enter SIR PETER

SIR PETER. When an old Bachelor takes a young Wife---what is He to expect---'Tis now six months since Lady Teazle made me the happiest of men---and I have been the most miserable Dog ever since that ever committed wedlock. We tift a little going to church---and came to a Quarrel before the Bells had done ringing---I was more than once nearly chok'd with gall during the Honeymoon---and had lost all comfort in Life before my Friends had done wishing me Joy--- yet I chose with caution---a girl bred wholly in the country---who never knew luxury beyond one silk gown---nor dissipation above the annual Gala of a Race-Ball---Yet she now plays her Part in all the extravagant Fopperies of the Fashion and the Town, with as ready a Grace as if she had never seen a Bush nor a grass Plot out of Grosvenor-Square! I am sneered at by my old acquaintance---paragraphed---in the news Papers---She dissipates my Fortune, and contradicts all my Humours---yet the worst of it is I doubt I love her or I should never bear all this. However I'll never be weak enough to own it.

Enter ROWLEY

ROWLEY. Sir Peter, your servant:---how is 't with you Sir---

SIR PETER. Very bad---Master Rowley---very bad[.] I meet with nothing but crosses and vexations---

ROWLEY. What can have happened to trouble you since yesterday?

SIR PETER. A good---question to a married man---

ROWLEY. Nay I'm sure your Lady Sir Peter can't be the cause of your uneasiness.

SIR PETER. Why has anybody told you she was dead[?]

ROWLEY. Come, come, Sir Peter, you love her, notwithstanding your tempers do not exactly agree.

SIR PETER. But the Fault is entirely hers, Master Rowley---I am myself, the sweetest temper'd man alive, and hate a teasing temper; and so I tell her a hundred Times a day---

ROWLEY. Indeed!

SIR PETER. Aye and what is very extraordinary in all our disputes she is always in the wrong! But Lady Sneerwell, and the Set she meets at her House, encourage the perverseness of her Disposition---then to complete my vexations---Maria---my Ward---whom I ought to have the Power of a Father over, is determined to turn Rebel too and absolutely refuses the man whom I have long resolved on for her husband---meaning I suppose, to bestow herself on his profligate Brother.

ROWLEY. You know Sir Peter I have always taken the Liberty to differ with you on the subject of these two young Gentlemen---I only wish you may not be deceived in your opinion of the elder. For Charles, my life on't! He will retrieve his errors yet---their worthy Father, once my honour'd master, was at his years nearly as wild a spark.

SIR PETER. You are wrong, Master Rowley---on their Father's Death you know I acted as a kind of Guardian to them both---till their uncle Sir Oliver's Eastern Bounty gave them an early independence. Of course no person could have more opportunities of judging of their Hearts---and I was never mistaken in my life. Joseph is indeed a model for the young men of the Age---He is a man of Sentiment---and acts up to the Sentiments he professes---but for the other[,] take my word for't [if] he had any grain of Virtue by descent---he has dissipated it with the rest of his inheritance. Ah! my old Friend, Sir Oliver will be deeply mortified when he finds how Part of his Bounty has been misapplied.

ROWLEY. I am sorry to find you so violent against the young man because this may be the most critical Period of his Fortune. I came hither with news that will surprise you.

SIR PETER. What! let me hear---

ROWLEY. Sir Oliver is arrived and at this moment in Town.

SIR PETER. How!---you astonish me---I thought you did not expect him this month!---

ROWLEY. I did not---but his Passage has been remarkably quick.

SIR PETER. Egad I shall rejoice to see my old Friend---'Tis sixteen years since we met---We have had many a Day together---but does he still enjoin us not to inform his Nephews of his Arrival?

ROWLEY. Most strictly---He means, before He makes it known to make some trial of their Dispositions and we have already planned something for the purpose.

SIR PETER. Ah there needs no art to discover their merits---however he shall have his way---but pray does he know I am married!

ROWLEY. Yes and will soon wish you joy.

SIR PETER. You may tell him 'tis too late---ah Oliver will laugh at me---we used to rail at matrimony together---but He has been steady to his Text---well He must be at my house tho'---I'll instantly give orders for his Reception---but Master Rowley---don't drop a word that Lady Teazle and I ever disagree.

ROWLEY. By no means.

SIR PETER. For I should never be able to stand Noll's jokes; so I'd have him think that we are a very happy couple.

ROWLEY. I understand you---but then you must be very careful not to differ while He's in the House with you.

SIR PETER. Egad---and so we must---that's impossible. Ah! Master Rowley when an old Batchelor marries a young wife---He deserves---no the crime carries the Punishment along with it.
[Exeunt.]

    END OF THE FIRST ACT

ACT II

SCENE I.---SIR PETER and LADY TEAZLE

SIR PETER. Lady Teazle---Lady Teazle I'll not bear it.

LADY TEAZLE. Sir Peter---Sir Peter you---may scold or smile, according to your Humour[,] but I ought to have my own way in everything, and what's more I will too---what! tho' I was educated in the country I know very well that women of Fashion in London are accountable to nobody after they are married.

SIR PETER. Very well! ma'am very well! so a husband is to have no influence, no authority?

LADY TEAZLE. Authority! no, to be sure---if you wanted authority over me, you should have adopted me and not married me[:] I am sure you were old enough.

SIR PETER. Old enough---aye there it is---well---well---Lady Teazle, tho' my life may be made unhappy by your Temper---I'll not be ruined by your extravagance---

LADY TEAZLE. My extravagance! I'm sure I'm not more extravagant than a woman of Fashion ought to be.

SIR PETER. No no Madam, you shall throw away no more sums on such unmeaning Luxury---'Slife to spend as much to furnish your Dressing Room with Flowers in winter as would suffice to turn the Pantheon into a Greenhouse, and give a Fete Champetre at Christmas.

LADY TEAZLE. Lord! Sir Peter am I to blame because Flowers are dear in cold weather? You should find fault with the Climate, and not with me. For my Part I'm sure I wish it was spring all the year round---and that Roses grew under one's Feet!

SIR PETER. Oons! Madam---if you had been born to those Fopperies I shouldn't wonder at your talking thus;---but you forget what your situation was when I married you---

LADY TEAZLE. No, no, I don't---'twas a very disagreeable one or I should never nave married you.

SIR PETER. Yes, yes, madam, you were then in somewhat a humbler Style---the daughter of a plain country Squire. Recollect Lady Teazle when I saw you first---sitting at your tambour in a pretty figured linen gown---with a Bunch of Keys at your side, and your apartment hung round with Fruits in worsted, of your own working---

LADY TEAZLE. O horrible!---horrible!---don't put me in mind of it!

SIR PETER. Yes, yes Madam and your daily occupation to inspect the Dairy, superintend the Poultry, make extracts from the Family Receipt-book, and comb your aunt Deborah's Lap Dog.

LADY TEAZLE. Abominable!

SIR PETER. Yes Madam---and what were your evening amusements? to draw Patterns for Ruffles, which you hadn't the materials to make---play Pope Joan with the Curate---to read a sermon to your Aunt---or be stuck down to an old Spinet to strum your father to sleep after a Fox Chase.

LADY TEAZLE. Scandalous---Sir Peter not a word of it true---

SIR PETER. Yes, Madam---These were the recreations I took you from---and now---no one more extravagantly in the Fashion---Every Fopery adopted---a head-dress to o'er top Lady Pagoda with feathers pendant horizontal and perpendicular---you forget[,] Lady Teazle---when a little wired gauze with a few Beads made you a fly Cap not much bigger than a blew-bottle, and your Hair was comb'd smooth over a Roll---

LADY TEAZLE. Shocking! horrible Roll!!

SIR PETER. But now---you must have your coach---Vis-a-vis, and three powder'd Footmen before your Chair---and in the summer a pair of white cobs to draw you to Kensington Gardens---no recollection when y ou were content to ride double, behind the Butler, on a docked Coach-Horse?

LADY TEAZLE. Horrid!---I swear I never did.

SIR PETER. This, madam, was your situation---and what have I not done for you? I have made you woman of Fashion of Fortune of Rank---in short I have made you my wife.

LADY TEAZLE. Well then and there is but one thing more you can make me to add to the obligation.

SIR PETER. What's that pray?

LADY TEAZLE. Your widow.---

SIR PETER. Thank you Madam---but don't flatter yourself for though your ill-conduct may disturb my Peace it shall never break my Heart I promise you---however I am equally obliged to you for the Hint.

LADY TEAZLE. Then why will you endeavour to make yourself so disagreeable to me---and thwart me in every little elegant expense.

SIR PETER. 'Slife---Madam I pray, had you any of these elegant expenses when you married me?

LADY TEAZLE. Lud Sir Peter would you have me be out of the Fashion?

SIR PETER. The Fashion indeed!---what had you to do with the Fashion before you married me?

LADY TEAZLE. For my Part---I should think you would like to have your wife thought a woman of Taste---

SIR PETER. Aye there again---Taste! Zounds Madam you had no Taste when you married me---

LADY TEAZLE. That's very true indeed Sir Peter! after having married you I should never pretend to Taste again I allow.

SIR PETER. So---so then---Madam---if these are your Sentiments pray how came I to be honour'd with your Hand?

LADY TEAZLE. Shall I tell you the Truth?

SIR PETER. If it's not too great a Favour.

LADY TEAZLE. Why the Fact is I was tired of all those agreeable Recreations which you have so good naturally [naturedly] Described---and having a Spirit to spend and enjoy a Fortune---I determined to marry the first rich man that would have me.

SIR PETER. A very honest confession---truly---but pray madam was there no one else you might have tried to ensnare but me.

LADY TEAZLE. O lud---I drew my net at several but you were the only one I could catch.

SIR PETER. This is plain dealing indeed---

LADY TEAZLE. But now Sir Peter if we have finish'd our daily Jangle I presume I may go to my engagement at Lady Sneerwell's?

SIR PETER. Aye---there's another Precious circumstance---a charming set of acquaintance---you have made there!

LADY TEAZLE. Nay Sir Peter they are People of Rank and Fortune---and remarkably tenacious of reputation.

SIR PETER. Yes egad they are tenacious of Reputation with a vengeance, for they don't chuse anybody should have a Character but themselves! Such a crew! Ah! many a wretch has rid on hurdles who has done less mischief than these utterers of forged Tales, coiners of Scandal, and clippers of Reputation.

LADY TEAZLE. What would you restrain the freedom of speech?

SIR PETER. Aye they have made you just as bad [as] any one of the Society.

LADY TEAZLE. Why---I believe I do bear a Part with a tolerable Grace---But I vow I bear no malice against the People I abuse, when I say an ill-natured thing, 'tis out of pure Good Humour--- and I take it for granted they deal exactly in the same manner with me, but Sir Peter you know you promised to come to Lady Sneerwell's too.

SIR PETER. Well well I'll call in, just to look after my own character.

LADY TEAZLE. Then, indeed, you must make Haste after me, or you'll be too late---so good bye to ye.

SIR PETER. So---I have gain'd much by my intended expostulation---yet with what a charming air she contradicts every thing I say---and how pleasingly she shows her contempt of my authority---Well tho' I can't make her love me, there is certainly a great satisfaction in quarrelling with her; and I think she never appears to such advantage as when she is doing everything in her Power to plague me.

[Exit.]

SCENE II.---At LADY SNEERWELL'S

LADY SNEERWELL, MRS. CANDOUR, CRABTREE, SIR BENJAMIN BACKBITE,
    and SURFACE

LADY SNEERWELL. Nay, positively, we will hear it.

SURFACE. Yes---yes the Epigram by all means.

SiR BENJAMIN. O plague on't unkle---'tis mere nonsense---

CRABTREE. No no; 'fore gad very clever for an extempore!

SIR BENJAMIN. But ladies you should be acquainted with the circumstances. You must know that one day last week as Lady Betty Curricle was taking the Dust in High Park, in a sort of duodecimo Phaeton---she desired me to write some verses on her Ponies---upon which I took out my Pocket-Book---and in one moment produced---the following:---

'Sure never were seen two such beautiful Ponies;
    Other Horses are Clowns---and these macaronies,
    Nay to give 'em this Title, I'm sure isn't wrong,
    Their Legs are so slim---and their Tails are so long.

CRABTREE. There Ladies---done in the smack of a whip and on Horseback too.

SURFACE. A very Phoebus, mounted---indeed Sir Benjamin.

SIR BENJAMIN. Oh dear Sir---Trifles---Trifles.

Enter LADY TEAZLE and MARIA

MRS. CANDOUR. I must have a Copy---

LADY SNEERWELL. Lady Teazle---I hope we shall see Sir Peter?

LADY TEAZLE. I believe He'll wait on your Ladyship presently.

LADY SNEERWELL. Maria my love you look grave. Come, you sit down to Piquet with Mr. Surface.

MARIA. I take very little Pleasure in cards---however, I'll do as you Please.

LADY TEAZLE. I am surprised Mr. Surface should sit down her---I thought He would have embraced this opportunity of speaking to me before Sir Peter came---[Aside.]

MRS. CANDOUR. Now, I'll die but you are so scandalous I'll forswear your society.

LADY TEAZLE. What's the matter, Mrs. Candour?

MRS. CANDOUR. They'll not allow our friend Miss Vermillion to be handsome.

LADY SNEERWELL. Oh, surely she is a pretty woman. . . .

[CRABTREE.] I am very glad you think so ma'am.

MRS. CANDOUR. She has a charming fresh Colour.

CRABTREE. Yes when it is fresh put on---

LADY TEAZLE. O fie! I'll swear her colour is natural---I have seen it come and go---

CRABTREE. I dare swear you have, ma'am: it goes of a Night, and comes again in the morning.

SIR BENJAMIN. True, uncle, it not only comes and goes but what's more egad her maid can fetch and carry it---

MRS. CANDOUR. Ha! ha! ha! how I hate to hear you talk so! But surely, now, her Sister, is or was very handsome.

CRABTREE. Who? Mrs. Stucco? O lud! she's six-and-fifty if she's an hour!

MRS. CANDOUR. Now positively you wrong her[;] fifty-two, or fifty-three is the utmost---and I don't think she looks more.

SIR BENJAMIN. Ah! there's no judging by her looks, unless one was to see her Face.

LADY SNEERWELL. Well---well---if she does take some pains to repair the ravages of Time--- you must allow she effects it with great ingenuity---and surely that's better than the careless manner in which the widow Ocre chaulks her wrinkles.

SIR BENJAMIN. Nay now---you are severe upon the widow---come---come, it isn't that she paints so ill---but when she has finished her Face she joins it on so badly to her Neck, that she looks like a mended Statue, in which the Connoisseur sees at once that the Head's modern tho' the Trunk's antique------

CRABTREE. Ha! ha! ha! well said, Nephew!

MRS. CANDOUR. Ha! ha! ha! Well, you make me laugh but I vow I hate you for it---what do you think of Miss Simper?

SIR BENJAMIN. Why, she has very pretty Teeth.

LADY TEAZLE. Yes and on that account, when she is neither speaking nor laughing (which very seldom happens)---she never absolutely shuts her mouth, but leaves it always on a-Jar, as it were------

MRS. CANDOUR. How can you be so ill-natured!

LADY TEAZLE. Nay, I allow even that's better than the Pains Mrs. Prim takes to conceal her losses in Front---she draws her mouth till it resembles the aperture of a Poor's-Box, and all her words appear to slide out edgewise.

LADY SNEERWELL. Very well Lady Teazle I see you can be a little severe.

LADY TEAZLE. In defence of a Friend it is but justice, but here comes Sir Peter to spoil our Pleasantry.

Enter SIR PETER

SIR PETER. Ladies, your obedient---Mercy on me---here is the whole set! a character's dead at every word, I suppose.

MRS. CANDOUR. I am rejoiced you are come, Sir Peter---they have been so censorious and Lady Teazle as bad as any one.

SIR PETER. That must be very distressing to you, Mrs. Candour I dare swear.

MRS. CANDOUR. O they will allow good Qualities to nobody---not even good nature to our Friend Mrs. Pursy.

LADY TEAZLE. What, the fat dowager who was at Mrs. Codrille's [Quadrille's] last Night?

LADY SNEERWELL. Nay---her bulk is her misfortune and when she takes such Pains to get rid of it you ought not to reflect on her.

MRS. CANDOUR. 'Tis very true, indeed.

LADY TEAZLE. Yes, I know she almost lives on acids and small whey---laces herself by pulleys and often in the hottest noon of summer you may see her on a little squat Pony, with her hair plaited up behind like a Drummer's and puffing round the Ring on a full trot.

MRS. CANDOUR. I thank you Lady Teazle for defending her.

SIR PETER. Yes, a good Defence, truly!

MRS. CANDOUR. But for Sir Benjamin, He is as censorious as Miss Sallow.

CRABTREE. Yes and she is a curious Being to pretend to be censorious---an awkward Gawky, without any one good Point under Heaven!

LADY SNEERWELL. Positively you shall not be so very severe. Miss Sallow is a Relation of mine by marriage, and, as for her Person great allowance is to be made---for, let me tell you a woman labours under many disadvantages who tries to pass for a girl at six-and-thirty.

MRS. CANDOUR. Tho', surely she is handsome still---and for the weakness in her eyes considering how much she reads by candle-light it is not to be wonder'd at.

LADY SNEERWELL. True and then as to her manner---upon my word I think it is particularly graceful considering she never had the least Education[:] for you know her Mother was a Welch milliner, and her Father a sugar-Baker at Bristow.---

SIR BENJAMIN. Ah! you are both of you too good-natured!

SIR PETER. Yes, damned good-natured! Her own relation! mercy on me! [Aside.]

MRS. CANDOUR. For my Part I own I cannot bear to hear a friend ill-spoken of?

SIR PETER. No, to be sure!

SIR BENJAMIN. Ah you are of a moral turn Mrs. Candour and can sit for an hour to hear Lady Stucco talk sentiments.

LADY SNEERWELL. Nay I vow Lady Stucco is very well with the Dessert after Dinner for she's just like the Spanish Fruit one cracks for mottoes---made up of Paint and Proverb.

MRS. CANDOUR. Well, I never will join in ridiculing a Friend---and so I constantly tell my cousin Ogle---and you all know what pretensions she has to be critical in Beauty.

LADY TEAZLE. O to be sure she has herself the oddest countenance that ever was seen---'tis a collection of Features from all the different Countries of the globe.

SIR BENJAMIN. So she has indeed---an Irish Front------

CRABTREE. Caledonian Locks------

SIR BENJAMIN. Dutch Nose------

CRABTREE. Austrian Lips------

SIR BENJAMIN. Complexion of a Spaniard------

CRABTREE. And Teeth a la Chinoise------

SIR BENJAMIN. In short, her Face resembles a table d'hote at Spa---where no two guests are of a nation------

CRABTREE. Or a Congress at the close of a general War---wherein all the members even to her eyes appear to have a different interest and her Nose and Chin are the only Parties likely to join issue.

MRS. CANDOUR. Ha! ha! ha!

SIR PETER. Mercy on my Life[!] a Person they dine with twice a week! [Aside.]

LADY SNEERWELL. Go---go---you are a couple of provoking Toads.

MRS. CANDOUR. Nay but I vow you shall not carry the Laugh off so---for give me leave to say, that Mrs. Ogle------

SIR PETER. Madam---madam---I beg your Pardon---there's no stopping these good Gentlemen's Tongues---but when I tell you Mrs. Candour that the Lady they are abusing is a particular Friend of mine, I hope you'll not take her Part.

LADY SNEERWELL. Ha! ha! ha! well said, Sir Peter---but you are a cruel creature---too Phlegmatic yourself for a jest and too peevish to allow wit in others.

SIR PETER. Ah Madam true wit is more nearly allow'd [allied?] to good Nature than your Ladyship is aware of.

LADY SNEERWELL. True Sir Peter---I believe they are so near akin that they can never be united.

SIR BENJAMIN. O rather Madam suppose them man and wife because one seldom sees them together.

LADY TEAZLE. But Sir Peter is such an Enemy to Scandal I believe He would have it put down by Parliament.

SIR PETER. 'Fore heaven! Madam, if they were to consider the Sporting with Reputation of as much importance as poaching on manors---and pass an Act for the Preservation of Fame---there are many would thank them for the Bill.

LADY SNEERWELL. O Lud! Sir Peter would you deprive us of our Privileges---

SIR PETER. Aye Madam---and then no person should be permitted to kill characters or run down reputations, but qualified old Maids and disappointed Widows.---

LADY SNEERWELL. Go, you monster---

MRS. CANDOUR. But sure you would not be quite so severe on those who only report what they hear?

SIR PETER. Yes Madam, I would have Law Merchant for that too---and in all cases of slander currency, whenever the Drawer of the Lie was not to be found, the injured Party should have a right to come on any of the indorsers.

CRABTREE. Well for my Part I believe there never was a Scandalous Tale without some foundation.3

LADY SNEERWELL. Come Ladies shall we sit down to Cards in the next Room?

Enter SERVANT, whispers SIR PETER

SIR PETER. I'll be with them directly.---

[Exit SERVANT.]

I'll get away unperceived.

LADY SNEERWELL. Sir Peter you are not leaving us?

SIR PETER. Your Ladyship must excuse me---I'm called away by particular Business---but I leave my Character behind me---

[Exit.]

SIR BENJAMIN. Well certainly Lady Teazle that lord of yours is a strange being---I could tell you some stories of him would make you laugh heartily if He wern't your Husband.

LADY TEAZLE. O pray don't mind that---come do let's hear 'em.

[join the rest of the Company going into the Next Room.]

SURFACE. Maria I see you have no satisfaction in this society.

MARIA. How is it possible I should? If to raise malicious smiles at the infirmities or misfortunes of those who have never injured us be the province of wit or Humour, Heaven grant me a double Portion of Dullness---

SURFACE. Yet they appear more ill-natured than they are---they have no malice at heart---

MARIA. Then is their conduct still more contemptible[;] for in my opinion---nothing could excuse the intemperance of their tongues but a natural and ungovernable bitterness of Mind.

SURFACE. Undoubtedly Madam---and it has always been a sentiment of mine---that to propagate a malicious Truth wantonly---is more despicable than to falsify from Revenge, but can you Maria feel thus [f]or others and be unkind to me alone---nay is hope to be denied the tenderest Passion.---

MARIA. Why will you distress me by renewing this subject---

SURFACE. Ah! Maria! you would not treat me thus and oppose your guardian's Sir Peter's wishes---but that I see that my Profligate Brother is still a favour'd Rival.

MARIA. Ungenerously urged---but whatever my sentiments of that unfortunate young man are, be assured I shall not feel more bound to give him up because his Distresses have sunk him so low as to deprive him of the regard even of a Brother.

SURFACE. Nay but Maria do not leave me with a Frown---by all that's honest, I swear------Gad's Life here's Lady Teazle---you must not---no you shall---for tho' I have the greatest Regard for

Lady Teazle------

MARIA. Lady Teazle!

SURFACE. Yet were Sir Peter to suspect------

[Enter LADY TEAZLE, and comes forward]

LADY TEAZLE. What's this, Pray---do you take her for me!---Child you are wanted in the next Room.---What's all this, pray---

SURFACE. O the most unlucky circumstance in Nature. Maria has somehow suspected the tender concern I have for your happiness, and threaten'd to acquaint Sir Peter with her suspicions---and I was just endeavouring to reason with her when you came.

LADY TEAZLE. Indeed but you seem'd to adopt---a very tender mode of reasoning---do you usually argue on your knees?

SURFACE. O she's a Child---and I thought a little Bombast------but Lady Teazle when are you to give me your judgment on my Library as you promised------

LADY TEAZLE. No---no I begin to think it would be imprudent---and you know I admit you as a Lover no farther than Fashion requires.

SURFACE. True---a mere Platonic Cicisbeo, what every London wife is entitled to.

LADY TEAZLE. Certainly one must not be out of the Fashion---however, I have so much of my country Prejudices left---that---though Sir Peter's ill humour may vex me ever so, it never shall provoke me to------

SURFACE. The only revenge in your Power---well I applaud your moderation.

LADY TEAZLE. Go---you are an insinuating Hypocrite---but we shall be miss'd---let us join the company.

SURFACE. True, but we had best not return together.

LADY TEAZLE. Well don't stay---for Maria shan't come to hear any more of your Reasoning, I promise you---

[Exit.]

SURFACE. A curious Dilemma truly my Politics have run me into. I wanted at first only to ingratiate myself with Lady Teazle that she might not be my enemy with Maria---and I have I don't know how---become her serious Lover, so that I stand a chance of Committing a Crime I never meditated---and probably of losing Maria by the Pursuit!---Sincerely I begin to wish I had never made such a Point of gaining so very good a character, for it has led me into so many curst Rogueries that I doubt I shall be exposed at last.

[Exit.]

SCENE III.---At SIR PETER'S

---ROWLEY and SIR OLIVER---

SIR OLIVER. Ha! ha! ha! and so my old Friend is married, hey?---a young wife out of the country!---ha! ha! that he should have stood Bluff to old Bachelor so long and sink into a Husband at last!

ROWLEY. But you must not rally him on the subject Sir Oliver---'tis a tender Point I assure you though He has been married only seven months.

SIR OLIVER. Ah then he has been just half a year on the stool of Repentance---Poor Peter! But you say he has entirely given up Charles---never sees him, hey?

ROWLEY. His Prejudice against him is astonishing---and I am sure greatly increased by a jealousy of him with Lady Teazle---which he has been industriously led into by a scandalous Society---in the neighbourhood---who have contributed not a little to Charles's ill name. Whereas the truth is[,] I believe[,] if the lady is partial to either of them his Brother is the Favourite.

SIR OLIVER. Aye---I know---there are a set of malicious prating prudent Gossips both male and Female, who murder characters to kill time, and will rob a young Fellow of his good name before He has years to know the value of it. . . but I am not to be prejudiced against my nephew by such I promise you! No! no---if Charles has done nothing false or mean, I shall compound for his extravagance.

ROWLEY. Then my life on't, you will reclaim him. Ah, Sir, it gives me new vigour to find that your heart is not turned against him---and that the son of my good old master has one friend however left---

SIR OLIVER. What! shall I forget Master Rowley---when I was at his house myself---egad my Brother and I were neither of us very prudent youths---and yet I believe you have not seen many better men than your old master was[.]

ROWLEY. 'Tis this Reflection gives me assurance that Charles may yet be a credit to his Family---but here comes Sir Peter------

SIR OLIVER. Egad so He does---mercy on me---He's greatly altered---and seems to have a settled married look---one may read Husband in his Face at this Distance.---

Enter SIR PETER

SIR PETER. Ha! Sir Oliver---my old Friend---welcome to England---a thousand Times!

SIR OLIVER. Thank you---thank you---Sir Peter---and Efaith I am as glad to find you well[,] believe me---

SIR PETER. Ah! 'tis a long time since we met---sixteen year I doubt Sir Oliver---and many a cross accident in the Time---

SIR OLIVER. Aye I have had my share---but, what[!] I find you are married---hey my old Boy--- well---well it can't be help'd---and so I wish you joy with all my heart---

SIR PETER. Thank you---thanks Sir Oliver.---Yes, I have entered into the happy state but we'll not talk of that now.

SIR OLIVER. True true Sir Peter old Friends shouldn't begin on grievances at first meeting. No, no---

ROWLEY. Take care pray Sir------

SIR OLIVER. Well---so one of my nephews I find is a wild Rogue---hey?

SIR PETER. Wild!---oh! my old Friend---I grieve for your disappointment there---He's a lost

31

young man indeed---however his Brother will make you amends; Joseph is indeed what a youth should be---everybody in the world speaks well of him---

SIR OLIVER. I am sorry to hear it---he has too good a character to be an honest Fellow. Everybody speaks well of him! Psha! then He has bow'd as low to Knaves and Fools as to the honest dignity of Virtue.

SIR PETER. What Sir Oliver do you blame him for not making Enemies?

SIR OLIVER. Yes---if He has merit enough to deserve them.

SIR PETER. Well---well---you'll be convinced when you know him---'tis edification to hear him converse---he professes the noblest Sentiments.

SIR OLIVER. Ah plague on his Sentiments---if he salutes me with a scrap sentence of morality in his mouth I shall be sick directly---but however don't mistake me Sir Peter I don't mean to defend Charles's Errors---but before I form my judgment of either of them, I intend to make a trial of their Hearts---and my Friend Rowley and I have planned something for the Purpose.

ROWLEY. And Sir Peter shall own he has been for once mistaken.

SIR PETER. My life on Joseph's Honour------

SIR OLIVER. Well come give us a bottle of good wine---and we'll drink the Lads' Healths and tell you our scheme.

SIR PETER. Alons [Allons], then------

SIR OLIVER. But don't Sir Peter be so severe against your old Friend's son.

SIR PETER. 'Tis his Vices and Follies have made me his Enemy.---

ROWLEY. Come---come---Sir Peter consider how early He was left to his own guidance.

SIR OLIVER. Odds my Life---I am not sorry that He has run out of the course a little---for my Part, I hate to see dry Prudence clinging to the green juices of youth---'tis like ivy round a sapling and spoils the growth of the Tree.

END OF THE SECOND ACT

ACT III

SCENE I.---At SIR PETER'S

SIR PETER, SIR OLIVER, and ROWLEY

SIR PETER. Well, then, we will see the Fellows first and have our wine afterwards.---but how is this, Master Rowley---I don't see the Jet of your scheme.

ROWLEY. Why Sir---this Mr. Stanley whom I was speaking of, is nearly related to them by their mother. He was once a merchant in Dublin---but has been ruined by a series of undeserved misfortunes---and now lately coming over to solicit the assistance of his friends here---has been flyng [flung] into prison by some of his Creditors---where he is now with two helpless Boys.---

SIR OLIVER. Aye and a worthy Fellow too I remember him. But what is this to lead to---?

ROWLEY. You shall hear---He has applied by letter both to Mr. Surface and Charles---from the former he has received nothing but evasive promises of future service, while Charles has done all that his extravagance has left him power to do---and He is at this time endeavouring to raise a sum of money---part of which, in the midst of his own distresses, I know He intends for the service of poor Stanley.

SIR OLIVER. Ah! he is my Brother's Son.

SIR PETER. Well, but how is Sir Oliver personally to------

ROWLEY. Why Sir I will inform Charles and his Brother that Stanley has obtain'd permission to apply in person to his Friends---and as they have neither of them ever seen him[,] let Sir Oliver assume his character---and he will have a fair opportunity of judging at least of the Benevolence of their Dispositions.

SIR PETER. Pshaw! this will prove nothing---I make no doubt Charles is Coxcomb and thoughtless enough to give money to poor relations if he had it---

SIR OLIVER. Then He shall never want it---. I have brought a few Rupees home with me Sir Peter---and I only want to be sure of bestowing them rightly.---

ROWLEY. Then Sir believe me you will find in the youngest Brother one who in the midst of Folly and dissipation---has still, as our immortal Bard expresses it,---

"a Tear for Pity and a Hand open as the day for melting Charity."

SIR PETER. Pish! What signifies his having an open Hand or Purse either when He has nothing left to give!---but if you talk of humane Sentiments---Joseph is the man---Well, well, make the trial, if you please. But where is the fellow whom you brought for Sir Oliver to examine, relative to Charles's affairs?

ROWLEY. Below waiting his commands, and no one can give him better intelligence---This, Sir Oliver, is a friendly Jew, who to do him justice, has done everything in his power to bring your nephew to a proper sense of his extravagance.

SIR PETER. Pray let us have him in.

ROWLEY. Desire Mr. Moses to walk upstairs.

[Calls to SERVANT.]

SIR PETER. But Pray why should you suppose he will speak the truth?

ROWLEY. Oh, I have convinced him that he has no chance of recovering certain Sums advanced to Charles but through the bounty of Sir Oliver, who He knows is arrived; so that you may depend on his Fidelity to his interest. I have also another evidence in my Power, one Snake, whom I shall shortly produce to remove some of YOUR Prejudices[,] Sir Peter[,] relative to Charles and Lady Teazle.

SIR PETER. I have heard too much on that subject.

ROWLEY. Here comes the honest Israelite.

Enter MOSES

---This is Sir Oliver.

SIR OLIVER. Sir---I understand you have lately had great dealings with my Nephew Charles.

MOSES. Yes Sir Oliver---I have done all I could for him, but He was ruined before He came to me for Assistance.

SIR OLIVER. That was unlucky truly---for you have had no opportunity of showing your Talents.

MOSES. None at all---I hadn't the Pleasure of knowing his Distresses till he was some thousands worse than nothing, till it was impossible to add to them.

SIR OLIVER. Unfortunate indeed! but I suppose you have done all in your Power for him honest Moses?

MOSES. Yes he knows that---This very evening I was to have brought him a gentleman from the city who does not know him and will I believe advance some money.

SIR PETER. What[!] one Charles has never had money from before?

MOSES. Yes[---]Mr. Premium, of Crutched Friars.

SIR PETER. Egad, Sir Oliver a Thought strikes me!---Charles you say does'nt know Mr. Premium?

MOSES. Not at all.

SIR PETER. Now then Sir Oliver you may have a better opportunity of satisfying yourself than by an old romancing tale of a poor Relation---go with my friend Moses and represent Mr. Premium and then I'll answer for't you'll see your Nephew in all his glory.

SIR OLIVER. Egad I like this Idea better than the other, and I may visit Joseph afterwards as old Stanley.

SIR PETER. True so you may.

ROWLEY. Well this is taking Charles rather at a disadvantage, to be sure---however Moses---you understand Sir Peter and will be faithful------

MOSES. You may depend upon me---and this is near the Time I was to have gone.

SIR OLIVER. I'll accompany you as soon as you please, Moses------but hold---I have forgot one thing---how the plague shall I be able to pass for a Jew?

MOSES. There's no need---the Principal is Christian.

SIR OLIVER. Is He---I'm very sorry to hear it---but then again---an't I rather too smartly dressed to look like a money-Lender?

SIR PETER. Not at all; 'twould not be out of character, if you went in your own carriage---would it, Moses!

MOSES. Not in the least.

SIR OLIVER. Well---but---how must I talk[?] there's certainly some cant of usury and mode of treating that I ought to know.

SIR PETER. Oh, there's not much to learn---the great point as I take it is to be exorbitant enough

36

in your Demands hey Moses?

MOSES. Yes that's very great Point.

SIR OLIVER. I'll answer for't I'll not be wanting in that---I'll ask him eight or ten per cent. on the loan---at least.

MOSES. You'll be found out directly---if you ask him no more than that, you'll be discovered immediately.

SIR OLIVER. Hey!---what the Plague!---how much then?

MOSES. That depends upon the Circumstances---if he appears not very anxious for the supply, you should require only forty or fifty per cent.---but if you find him in great Distress, and want the monies very bad---you may ask double.

SIR PETER. A good---[h]onest Trade you're learning, Sir Oliver---

SIR OLIVER. Truly, I think so---and not unprofitable---

MOSES. Then you know---you haven't the monies yourself, but are forced to borrow them for him of a Friend.

SIR OLIVER. O I borrow it of a Friend do I?

MOSES. And your friend is an unconscion'd Dog---but you can't help it.

SIR OLIVER. My Friend's an unconscionable Dog, is he?

MOSES. Yes---and He himself hasn't the monies by him---but is forced to sell stock---at a great loss---

SIR OLIVER. He is forced to sell stock is he---at a great loss, is he---well that's very kind of him---

SIR PETER. Efaith, Sir Oliver---Mr. Premium I mean---you'll soon be master of the Trade---but, Moses would have him inquire if the borrower is a minor---

MOSES. O yes---

SIR PETER. And in that case his Conscience will direct him---

MOSES. To have the Bond in another Name to be sure.

SIR OLIVER. Well---well I shall be perfect---

SIR PETER. But hearkee wouldn't you have him also run out a little against the annuity Bill---that would be in character I should think---

MOSES. Very much---

ROWLEY. And lament that a young man now must be at years of discretion before He is suffered to ruin himself!

MOSES. Aye, great Pity!

SIR PETER. And abuse the Public for allowing merit to an act whose only object is to snatch misfortune and imprudence from the rapacious Relief of usury! and give the minor a chance of inheriting his estate without being undone by coming into Possession.

SIR OLIVER. So---so---Moses shall give me further instructions as we go together.

SIR PETER. You will not have much time[,] for your Nephew lives hard bye---

SIR OLIVER. Oh Never---fear[:] my Tutor appears so able that tho' Charles lived in the next street it must be my own Fault if I am not a compleat Rogue before I turn the Corner---

[Exeunt SIR OLIVER and MOSES.]

SIR PETER. So---now I think Sir Oliver will be convinced---you shan't follow them Rowley. You are partial and would have prepared Charles for 'tother plot.

ROWLEY. No upon my word Sir Peter---

SIR PETER. Well, go bring me this Snake, and I'll hear what he has to say presently. I see Maria, and want to speak with her.---

[Exit ROWLEY.]

I should be glad to be convinced my suspicions of Lady Teazle and Charles were unjust---I have never yet opened my mind on this subject to my Friend Joseph. . . . I am determined. I will do it---He will give me his opinion sincerely.---

Enter MARIA

So Child---has Mr. Surface returned with you---

MARIA. No Sir---He was engaged.

SIR PETER. Well---Maria---do you not reflect[,] the more you converse with that amiable young man[,] what return his Partiality for you deserves?

MARIA. Indeed Sir Peter---your frequent importunity on this subject distresses me extremely--- you compell me to Declare that I know no man who has ever paid me a particular Attention whom I would not prefer to Mr. Surface---

SIR PETER. Soh! Here's Perverseness---no---no---Maria, 'tis Charles only whom you would prefer---'tis evident his Vices and Follies have won your Heart.

MARIA. This is unkind Sir---You know I have obey'd you in neither seeing nor corresponding with him---I have heard enough to convince me that He is unworthy my regard---Yet I cannot think it culpable---if while my understanding severely condemns his Vices, my Heart suggests some Pity for his Distresses.

SIR PETER. Well well pity him as much as you please, but give your Heart and Hand to a worthier object.

MARIA. Never to his Brother!

SIR PETER. Go---perverse and obstinate! but take care, Madam---you have never yet known what the authority of a Guardian is---don't compel me to inform you of it.---

MARIA. I can only say, you shall not have just Reason---'tis true, by my Father's will I am for a short period bound to regard you as his substitute, but I must cease to think you so when you would compel me to be miserable.

[Exit.]

SIR PETER. Was ever man so crossed as I am[?] everything conspiring to fret me! I had not been involved in matrimony a fortnight[,] before her Father---a hale and hearty man, died on purpose, I believe---for the Pleasure of plaguing me with the care of his Daughter . . . but here comes my Helpmate!---She appears in great good humour------how happy I should be if I could teaze her into loving me tho' but a little------

Enter LADY TEAZLE

LADY TEAZLE. Lud! Sir Peter I hope you haven't been quarrelling with Maria? It isn't using me well to be ill humour'd when I am not bye---!

SIR PETER. Ah! Lady Teazle you might have the Power to make me good humour'd at all times---

LADY TEAZLE. I am sure---I wish I had---for I want you to be in a charming sweet temper at this moment---do be good humour'd now---and let me have two hundred Pounds will you?

SIR PETER. Two hundred Pounds! what an't I to be in a good humour without paying for it---but speak to me thus---and Efaith there's nothing I could refuse you. You shall have it---but seal me a bond for the repayment.

LADY TEAZLE. O no---there---my Note of Hand will do as well---

SIR PETER. And you shall no longer reproach me with not giving you an independent settlement---I shall shortly surprise you---and you'll not call me ungenerous---but shall we always live thus---hey?

LADY TEAZLE. If you---please---I'm sure I don't care how soon we leave off quarrelling provided you'll own you were tired first---

SIR PETER. Well---then let our future contest be who shall be most obliging.

LADY TEAZLE. I assure you Sir Peter Good Nature becomes you---you look now as you did before we were married---when you used to walk with me under the Elms, and tell me stories of what a Gallant you were in your youth---and chuck me under the chin you would---and ask me if I thought I could love an old Fellow who would deny me nothing---didn't you?

SIR PETER. Yes---yes---and you were as kind and attentive------

LADY TEAZLE. Aye so I was---and would always take your Part, when my acquaintance used to abuse you and turn you into ridicule---

SIR PETER. Indeed!

LADY TEAZLE. Aye---and when my cousin Sophy has called you a stiff peevish old batchelor and laugh'd at me for thinking of marrying one who might be my Father---I have always defended you---and said I didn't think you so ugly by any means, and that you'd make a very good sort of a husband---

SIR PETER. And you prophesied right---and we shall certainly now be the happiest couple------

LADY TEAZLE. And never differ again.

SIR PETER. No never---tho' at the same time indeed---my dear Lady Teazle---you must watch your Temper very narrowly---for in all our little Quarrels---my dear---if you recollect my Love you always began first---

LADY TEAZLE. I beg your Pardon---my dear Sir Peter---indeed---you always gave the provocation.

SIR PETER. Now---see, my Love take care---contradicting isn't the way to keep Friends.

LADY TEAZLE. Then don't you begin it my Love!

SIR PETER. There now---you are going on---you don't perceive[,] my Life, that you are just doing the very thing my Love which you know always makes me angry.

LADY TEAZLE. Nay---you know if you will be angry without any reason---my Dear------

SIR PETER. There now you want to quarrel again.

LADY TEAZLE. No---I am sure I don't---but if you will be so peevish------

SIR PETER. There---now who begins first?

LADY TEAZLE. Why you to be sure---I said nothing[---]but there's no bearing your Temper.

SIR PETER. No---no---my dear---the fault's in your own temper.

LADY TEAZLE. Aye you are just what my Cousin Sophy said you would be---

SIR PETER. Your Cousin Sophy---is a forward impertinent Gipsey---

LADY TEAZLE. Go you great Bear---how dare you abuse my Relations---

SIR PETER. Now may all the Plagues of marriage be doubled on me, if ever I try to be Friends with you any more------

LADY TEAZLE. So much the Better.

SIR PETER. No---no Madam 'tis evident you never cared a pin for me---I was a madman to marry you---

LADY TEAZLE. And I am sure I was a Fooll to marry you---an old dangling Batchelor, who was single of [at] fifty---only because He never could meet with any one who would have him.

SIR PETER. Aye---aye---Madam---but you were pleased enough to listen to me---you never had such an offer before---

LADY TEAZLE. No---didn't I refuse Sir Jeremy Terrier---who everybody said would have been a better Match---for his estate is just as good as yours---and he has broke his Neck since we have been married!

SIR PETER. I have done with you Madam! You are an unfeeling---ungrateful---but there's an end of everything---I believe you capable of anything that's bad---Yes, Madam---I now believe the Reports relative to you and Charles---Madam---yes---Madam---you and Charles are---not without grounds------

LADY TEAZLE. Take---care Sir Peter---you had better not insinuate any such thing! I'll not be suspected without cause I promise you------

SIR PETER. Very---well---Madam---very well! a separate maintenance---as soon as you Please. Yes Madam or a Divorce---I'll make an example of myself for the Benefit of all old Batchelors--- Let us separate, Madam.

LADY TEAZLE. Agreed---agreed---and now---my dear Sir Peter we are of a mind again, we may be the happiest couple---and never differ again, you know---ha! ha!---Well you are going to be in a Passion I see---and I shall only interrupt you---so, bye! bye! hey---young Jockey try'd and countered.
[Exit.]

SIR PETER. Plagues and tortures! She pretends to keep her temper, can't I make her angry neither! O! I am the miserable fellow! But I'll not bear her presuming to keep her Temper---No she may break my Heart---but she shan't keep her Temper.
[Exit.]

SCENE II.---At CHARLES's House

Enter TRIP, MOSES, and SIR OLIVER

TRIP. Here Master Moses---if you'll stay a moment---I'll try whether Mr.------what's the Gentleman's Name?

SIR OLIVER. Mr.------Moses---what IS my name------

MOSES. Mr. Premium------

TRIP. Premium---very well.

[Exit TRIP---taking snuff.]

SIR OLIVER. To judge by the Servants---one wouldn't believe the master was ruin'd---but what---sure this was my Brother's House------

MOSES. Yes Sir Mr. Charles bought it of Mr. Joseph with the Furniture, Pictures, &c.---just as the old Gentleman left it---Sir Peter thought it a great piece of extravagance in him.

SIR OLIVER. In my mind the other's economy in selling it to him was more reprehensible by half.------

Enter TRIP

TRIP. My Master[,] Gentlemen[,] says you must wait, he has company, and can't speak with you yet.

SIR OLIVER. If he knew who it was wanted to see him, perhaps he wouldn't have sent such a Message.

TRIP. Yes---yes---Sir---He knows you are here---I didn't forget little Premium---no---no------

SIR OLIVER. Very well---and pray Sir what may be your Name?

TRIP. Trip Sir---my Name is Trip, at your Service.

SIR OLIVER. Well then Mr. Trip---I presume your master is seldom without company------

TRIP. Very seldom Sir---the world says ill-natured things of him but 'tis all malice---no man was ever better beloved---Sir he seldom sits down to dinner without a dozen particular Friends------

SIR OLIVER. He's very happy indeed---you have a pleasant sort of Place here I guess?

TRIP. Why yes---here are three or four of us pass our time agreeably enough---but then our wages are sometimes a little in arrear---and not very great either---but fifty Pounds a year and find our own Bags and Bouquets------

SIR OLIVER. Bags and Bouquets!---Halters and Bastinadoes! [Aside.]

TRIP. But a propos Moses---have you been able to get me that little Bill discounted?

SIR OLIVER. Wants to raise money too!---mercy on me! has his distresses, I warrant[,] like a Lord---and affects Creditors and Duns! [Aside.]

MOSES. 'Twas not be done, indeed------

TRIP. Good lack---you surprise me---My Friend Brush has indorsed it and I thought when he put his name at the Back of a Bill 'twas as good as cash.

MOSES. No 'twouldn't do.

TRIP. A small sum---but twenty Pound---harkee, Moses do you think you could get it me by way of annuity?

SIR OLIVER. An annuity! ha! ha! a Footman raise money by annuity---Well done Luxury egad! [Aside.]

MOSES. Who would you get to join with you?

TRIP. You know my Lord Applice---you have seen him however------

MOSES. Yes------

TRIP. You must have observed what an appearance he makes---nobody dresses better, nobody throws off faster---very well this Gentleman will stand my security.

MOSES. Well---but you must insure your Place.

TRIP. O with all my Heart---I'll insure my Place, and my Life too, if you please.

SIR OLIVER. It's more than I would your neck------

MOSES. But is there nothing you could deposit?

TRIP. Why nothing capital of my master's wardrobe has drop'd lately---but I could give you a mortgage on some of his winter Cloaths with equity of redemption before November or---you shall have the reversion---of the French velvet, or a post obit on the Blue and Silver---these I should think Moses---with a few Pair of Point Ruffles as a collateral security---hey, my little Fellow?

MOSES. Well well---we'll talk presently---we detain the Gentlemen------

SIR OLIVER. O pray don't let me interrupt Mr. Trip's Negotiation.

TRIP. Harkee---I heard the Bell---I believe, Gentlemen I can now introduce you---don't forget the annuity little Moses.

SIR OLIVER. If the man be a shadow of his Master this is the Temple of Dissipation indeed!

[Exeunt.]

SCENE III.---CHARLES, CARELESS, etc., etc.

At Table with Wine

CHARLES. 'Fore Heaven, 'tis true!---there is the great Degeneracy of the age---many of our acquaintance have Taste---Spirit, and Politeness---but plague on't they won't drink------

CARELESS. It is so indeed---Charles---they give into all the substantial Luxuries of the Table---and abstain from nothing but wine and wit---Oh, certainly society suffers by it intolerably---for now instead of the social spirit of Raillery that used to mantle over a glass of bright Burgundy their conversation is become just like the Spa water they drink which has all the Pertness and flatulence of champaine without its spirit or Flavour.

FIRST GENTLEMAN. But what are they to do who love Play better than wine------

CARELESS. True---there's Harry diets himself---for gaming and is now under a hazard Regimen.

CHARLES. Then He'll have the worst of it---what you wouldn't train a horse for the course by keeping him from corn---For my Part egad I am never so successful as when I'm a little---merry---let me throw on a Bottle of Champaine and I never lose---at least I never feel my losses which is exactly the same thing.

SECOND GENTLEMAN. Aye that may be---but it is as impossible to follow wine and play as to unite Love and Politics.

CHARLES. Pshaw---you may do both---Caesar made Love and Laws in a Breath---and was liked by the Senate as well as the Ladies---but no man can pretend to be a Believer in Love, who is an abjurer of wine---'tis the Test by which a Lover knows his own Heart---fill a dozen Bumpers to a dozen Beauties, and she that floats atop is the maid that has bewitched you.

CARELESS. Now then Charles---be honest and give us yours------

CHARLES. Why I have withheld her only in compassion to you---if I toast her you should give a round of her Peers, which is impossible! on earth!

CARELESS. O, then we'll find some canonized Vestals or heathen Goddesses that will do I warrant------

CHARLES. Here then---Bumpers---you Rogues---Bumpers! Maria---Maria------

FIRST GENTLEMAN. Maria who?

CHARLES. Oh, damn the Surname 'tis too formal to be register'd in Love's calendar---but now Careless beware---beware---we must have Beauty's superlative.

FIRST GENTLEMAN. Nay Never study[,] Careless---we'll stand to the Toast---tho' your mistress should want an eye---and you know you have a song will excuse you------

CARELESS. Egad so I have---and I'll give him the song instead of the Lady.------

SONG.---AND CHORUS---<u>4</u>

```
    Here's to the maiden of bashful fifteen;
       Here's to the widow of fifty;
    Here's to the flaunting extravagant quean,
       And here's to the housewife that's thrifty.
    Chorus.  Let the toast pass,---
                   Drink to the lass,
    I'll warrant she'll prove an excuse for a glass.

    Here's to the charmer whose dimples we prize;
       Now to the maid who has none, sir;
```

```
Here's to the girl with a pair of blue eyes,
    And here's to the nymph with but one, sir.
Chorus.  Let the toast pass, &c.

Here's to the maid with a bosom of snow:
    Now to her that's as brown as a berry:
Here's to the wife with a face full of woe,
    And now to the damsel that's merry.
Chorus.  Let the toast pass, &c.

For let 'em be clumsy, or let 'em be slim,
    Young or ancient, I care not a feather;
So fill a pint bumper quite up to the brim,
So fill up your glasses, nay, fill to the brim,
    And let us e'en toast them together.
Chorus.  Let the toast pass, &c.
```

[Enter TRIP whispers CHARLES]

SECOND GENTLEMAN. Bravo Careless---Ther's Toast and Sentiment too.

FIRST GENTLEMAN. E' faith there's infinite charity in that song.------

CHARLES. Gentlemen, you must excuse me a little.---Careless, take the Chair, will you?

CARELESS. Nay prithee, Charles---what now---this is one of your Peerless Beauties I suppose---has dropped in by chance?

CHARLES. No---Faith---to tell you the Truth 'tis a Jew and a Broker who are come by appointment.

CARELESS. O dam it let's have the Jew in.

FIRST GENTLEMAN. Aye and the Broker too by all means------

SECOND GENTLEMAN. Yes yes the Jew and the Broker.

CHARLES. Egad with all my Heart---Trip---bid the Gentlemen walk in---tho' there's one of them a Stranger I can tell you------

TRIP. What Sir---would you chuse Mr. Premium to come up with------

FIRST GENTLEMAN. Yes---yes Mr. Premium certainly.

CARELESS. To be sure---Mr. Premium---by all means Charles, let us give them some generous Burgundy, and perhaps they'll grow conscientious------

CHARLES. O, Hang 'em---no---wine does but draw forth a man's natural qualities; and to make them drink would only be to whet their Knavery.

Enter TRIP, SIR OLIVER, and MOSES

CHARLES. So---honest Moses---walk in---walk in pray Mr. Premium---that's the Gentleman's name isn't it Moses.

MOSES. Yes Sir.

CHARLES. Set chairs---Trim.---Sit down, Mr Premium.---Glasses Trim.---sit down Moses.---Come, Mr. Premium I'll give you a sentiment---Here's Success to Usury---Moses fill the Gentleman a bumper.

MOSES. Success to Usury!

CARELESS. Right Moses---Usury is Prudence and industry and deserves to succeed------

SIR OLIVER. Then Here is---all the success it deserves! [Drinks.]

CHARLES. Mr. Premium you and I are but strangers yet---but I hope we shall be better acquainted by and bye------

SIR OLIVER. Yes Sir hope we shall---more intimately perhaps than you'll wish.5 [Aside.]

CARELESS. No, no, that won't do! Mr. Premium, you have demurred at the toast, and must drink it in a pint bumper.

FIRST GENTLEMAN. A pint bumper, at least.

MOSES. Oh, pray, sir, consider---Mr. Premium's a gentleman.

CARELESS. And therefore loves good wine.

SECOND GENTLEMAN. Give Moses a quart glass---this is mutiny, and a high contempt for the chair.

CARELESS. Here, now for't! I'll see justice done, to the last drop of my bottle.

SIR OLIVER. Nay, pray, gentlemen---I did not expect this usage.

CHARLES. No, hang it, you shan't; Mr. Premium's a stranger.

SIR OLIVER. Odd! I wish I was well out of their company. [Aside.]

CARELESS. Plague on 'em then! if they won't drink, we'll not sit down with them. Come, Harry, the dice are in the next room.---Charles, you'll join us when you have finished your business with the gentlemen?

CHARLES. I will! I will!---

[Exeunt SIR HARRY BUMPER and GENTLEMEN; CARELESS following.] Careless.

CARELESS. [Returning.] Well!

CHARLES. Perhaps I may want you.

CARELESS. Oh, you know I am always ready: word, note, or bond, 'tis all the same to me. [Exit.]

MOSES. Sir, this is Mr. Premium, a gentleman of the strictest honour and secrecy; and always performs what he undertakes. Mr. Premium, this is------

CHARLES. Psha! have done. Sir, my friend Moses is a very honest fellow, but a little slow at expression: he'll be an hour giving us our titles. Mr. Premium, the plain state of the matter is this: I am an extravagant young fellow who wants to borrow money; you I take to be a prudent old fellow, who have got money to lend. I am blockhead enough to give fifty per cent. sooner than not have it! and you, I presume, are rogue enough to take a hundred if you can get it. Now, sir, you see we are acquainted at once, and may proceed to business without further ceremony.

SIR OLIVER. Exceeding frank, upon my word. I see, sir, you are not a man of many compliments.

CHARLES. Oh, no, sir! plain dealing in business I always think best.

SIR OLIVER. Sir, I like you the better for it. However, You are mistaken in one thing; I have no money to lend, but I believe I could procure some of a friend; but then he's an unconscionable dog. Isn't he, Moses? And must sell stock to accommodate you. Mustn't he, Moses!

MOSES. Yes, indeed! You know I always speak the truth, and scorn to tell a lie!

CHARLES. Right. People that speak truth generally do. But these are trifles, Mr. Premium. What! I know money isn't to be bought without paying for't!

SIR OLIVER. Well, but what security could you give? You have no land, I suppose?

CHARLES. Not a mole-hill, nor a twig, but what's in the bough pots out of the window!

SIR OLIVER. Nor any stock, I presume?

CHARLES. Nothing but live stock---and that's only a few pointers and ponies. But pray, Mr.

Premium, are you acquainted at all with any of my connections?

SIR OLIVER. Why, to say the truth, I am.

CHARLES. Then you must know that I have a devilish rich uncle in the East Indies, Sir Oliver Surface, from whom I have the greatest expectations?

SIR OLIVER. That you have a wealthy uncle, I have heard; but how your expectations will turn out is more, I believe, than you can tell.

CHARLES. Oh, no!---there can be no doubt. They tell me I'm a prodigious favourite, and that he talks of leaving me everything.

SIR OLIVER. Indeed! this is the first I've heard of it.

CHARLES. Yes, yes, 'tis just so. Moses knows 'tis true; don't you, Moses?

MOSES. Oh, yes! I'll swear to't.

SIR OLIVER. Egad, they'll persuade me presently I'm at Bengal. [Aside.]

CHARLES. Now I propose, Mr. Premium, if it's agreeable to you, a post-obit on Sir Oliver's life: though at the same time the old fellow has been so liberal to me, that I give you my word, I should be very sorry to hear that anything had happened to him.

SIR OLIVER. Not more than I should, I assure you. But the bond you mention happens to be just the worst security you could offer me---for I might live to a hundred and never see the principal.

CHARLES. Oh, yes, you would! the moment Sir Oliver dies, you know, you would come on me for the money.

SIR OLIVER. Then I believe I should be the most unwelcome dun you ever had in your life.

CHARLES. What! I suppose you're afraid that Sir Oliver is too good a life?

SIR OLIVER. No, indeed I am not; though I have heard he is as hale and healthy as any man of his years in Christendom.

CHARLES. There again, now, you are misinformed. No, no, the climate has hurt him considerably, poor uncle Oliver. Yes, yes, he breaks apace, I'm told---and is so much altered lately that his nearest relations would not know him.

SIR OLIVER. No! Ha! ha! ha! so much altered lately that his nearest relations would not know him! Ha! ha! ha! egad---ha! ha! ha!

CHARLES. Ha! ha!---you're glad to hear that, little Premium?

SIR OLIVER. No, no, I'm not.

CHARLES. Yes, yes, you are---ha! ha! ha!---you know that mends your chance.

SIR OLIVER. But I'm told Sir Oliver is coming over; nay, some say he is actually arrived.

CHARLES. Psha! sure I must know better than you whether he's come or not. No, no, rely on't he's at this moment at Calcutta. Isn't he, Moses?

MOSES. Oh, yes, certainly.

SIR OLIVER. Very true, as you say, you must know better than I, though I have it from pretty good authority. Haven't I, Moses?

MOSES. Yes, most undoubted!

SIR OLIVER. But, Sir, as I understand you want a few hundreds immediately, is there nothing you could dispose of?

CHARLES. How do you mean?

SIR OLIVER. For instance, now, I have heard that your father left behind him a great quantity of massy old plate.

CHARLES. O Lud! that's gone long ago. Moses can tell you how better than I can.

SIR OLIVER. [Aside.] Good lack! all the family race-cups and corporation-bowls!---[Aloud.] Then it was also supposed that his library was one of the most valuable and compact.

CHARLES. Yes, yes, so it was---vastly too much so for a private gentleman. For my part, I was always of a communicative disposition, so I thought it a shame to keep so much knowledge to myself.

SIR OLIVER. [Aside.] Mercy upon me! learning that had run in the family like an heir-loom!---[Aloud.] Pray, what has become of the books?

CHARLES. You must inquire of the auctioneer, Master Premium, for I don't believe even Moses can direct you.

MOSES. I know nothing of books.

SIR OLIVER. So, so, nothing of the family property left, I suppose?

CHARLES. Not much, indeed; unless you have a mind to the family pictures. I have got a room full of ancestors above: and if you have a taste for old paintings, egad, you shall have 'em a bargain!

SIR OLIVER. Hey! what the devil! sure, you wouldn't sell your forefathers, would you?

CHARLES. Every man of them, to the best bidder.

SIR OLIVER. What! your great-uncles and aunts?

CHARLES. Ay, and my great-grandfathers and grandmothers too.

SIR OLIVER. [Aside.] Now I give him up!---[Aloud.] What the plague, have you no bowels for your own kindred? Odd's life! do you take me for Shylock in the play, that you would raise money of me on your own flesh and blood?

CHARLES. Nay, my little broker, don't be angry: what need you care, if you have your money's worth?

SIR OLIVER. Well, I'll be the purchaser: I think I can dispose of the family canvas.---[Aside.] Oh, I'll never forgive him this! never!

Re-enter CARELESS

CARELESS. Come, Charles, what keeps you?

CHARLES. I can't come yet. I'faith, we are going to have a sale above stairs; here's little Premium will buy all my ancestors!

CARELESS. Oh, burn your ancestors!

CHARLES. No, he may do that afterwards, if he pleases. Stay, Careless, we want you: egad, you shall be auctioneer---so come along with us.

CARELESS. Oh, have with you, if that's the case. I can handle a hammer as well as a dice box! Going! going!

SIR OLIVER. Oh, the profligates! [Aside.]

CHARLES. Come, Moses, you shall be appraiser, if we want one. Gad's life, little Premium, you don't seem to like the business?

SIR OLIVER. Oh, yes, I do, vastly! Ha! ha! ha! yes, yes, I think it a rare joke to sell one's family by auction---ha! ha!---[Aside.] Oh, the prodigal!

CHARLES. To be sure! when a man wants money, where the plague should he get assistance, if he can't make free with his own relations?

[Exeunt.]

SIR OLIVER. I'll never forgive him; never! never!

END OF THE THIRD ACT

ACT IV

SCENE I.---A Picture Room in CHARLES SURFACE'S House

Enter CHARLES, SIR OLIVER, MOSES, and CARELESS

CHARLES. Walk in, gentlemen, pray walk in;---here they are, the family of the Surfaces, up to the Conquest.

SIR OLIVER. And, in my opinion, a goodly collection.

CHARLES. Ay, ay, these are done in the true spirit of portrait-painting; no volontiere grace or expression. Not like the works of your modern Raphaels, who give you the strongest resemblance, yet contrive to make your portrait independent of you; so that you may sink the original and not hurt the picture. No, no; the merit of these is the inveterate likeness---all stiff and awkward as the originals, and like nothing in human nature besides.

SIR OLIVER. Ah! we shall never see such figures of men again.

CHARLES. I hope not. Well, you see, Master Premium, what a domestic character I am; here I sit of an evening surrounded by my family. But come, get to your pulpit, Mr. Auctioneer; here's an old gouty chair of my grandfather's will answer the purpose.

CARELESS. Ay, ay, this will do. But, Charles, I haven't a hammer; and what's an auctioneer without his hammer?

CHARLES. Egad, that's true. What parchment have we here? Oh, our genealogy in full. [Taking pedigree down.] Here, Careless, you shall have no common bit of mahogany, here's the family tree for you, you rogue! This shall be your hammer, and now you may knock down my ancestors with their own pedigree.

SIR OLIVER. What an unnatural rogue!---an ex post facto parricide! [Aside.]

CARELESS. Yes, yes, here's a list of your generation indeed;---faith, Charles, this is the most convenient thing you could have found for the business, for 'twill not only serve as a hammer, but a catalogue into the bargain. Come, begin---A-going, a-going, a-going!

CHARLES. Bravo, Careless! Well, here's my great uncle, Sir Richard Ravelin, a marvellous good general in his day, I assure you. He served in all the Duke of Marlborough's wars, and got that cut over his eye at the battle of Malplaquet. What say you, Mr. Premium? look at him---there's a hero! not cut out of his feathers, as your modern clipped captains are, but enveloped in wig and regimentals, as a general should be. What do you bid?

SIR OLIVER. [Aside to Moses.] Bid him speak.

MOSES. Mr. Premium would have you speak.

CHARLES. Why, then, he shall have him for ten pounds, and I'm sure that's not dear for a staff-officer.

SIR OLIVER. [Aside.] Heaven deliver me! his famous uncle Richard for ten pounds!---[Aloud.] Very well, sir, I take him at that.

CHARLES. Careless, knock down my uncle Richard.---Here, now, is a maiden sister of his, my great-aunt Deborah, done by Kneller, in his best manner, and esteemed a very formidable likeness. There she is, you see, a shepherdess feeding her flock. You shall have her for five pounds ten---the sheep are worth the money.

SIR OLIVER. [Aside.] Ah! poor Deborah! a woman who set such a value on herself!---[Aloud.] Five pounds ten---she's mine.

CHARLES. Knock down my aunt Deborah! Here, now, are two that were a sort of cousins of theirs.---You see, Moses, these pictures were done some time ago, when beaux wore wigs, and the ladies their own hair.

SIR OLIVER. Yes, truly, head-dresses appear to have been a little lower in those days.

CHARLES. Well, take that couple for the same.

MOSES. 'Tis a good bargain.

CHARLES. Careless!---This, now, is a grandfather of my mother's, a learned judge, well known on the western circuit,---What do you rate him at, Moses?

MOSES. Four guineas.

CHARLES. Four guineas! Gad's life, you don't bid me the price of his wig.---Mr. Premium, you have more respect for the woolsack; do let us knock his lordship down at fifteen.

SIR OLIVER. By all means.

CARELESS. Gone!

CHARLES. And there are two brothers of his, William and Walter Blunt, Esquires, both members of Parliament, and noted speakers; and, what's very extraordinary, I believe, this is the first time they were ever bought or sold.

SIR OLIVER. That is very extraordinary, indeed! I'll take them at your own price, for the honour of Parliament.

CARELESS. Well said, little Premium! I'll knock them down at forty.

CHARLES. Here's a jolly fellow---I don't know what relation, but he was mayor of Norwich: take him at eight pounds.

SIR OLIVER. No, no; six will do for the mayor.

CHARLES. Come, make it guineas, and I'll throw you the two aldermen here into the bargain.

SIR OLIVER. They're mine.

CHARLES. Careless, knock down the mayor and aldermen. But, plague on't! we shall be all day retailing in this manner; do let us deal wholesale: what say you, little Premium? Give me three hundred pounds for the rest of the family in the lump.

CARELESS. Ay, ay, that will be the best way.

SIR OLIVER. Well, well, anything to accommodate you; they are mine. But there is one portrait which you have always passed over.

CARELESS. What, that ill-looking little fellow over the settee?

SIR OLIVER. Yes, sir, I mean that; though I don't think him so ill-looking a little fellow, by any means.

CHARLES. What, that? Oh; that's my uncle Oliver! 'Twas done before he went to India.

CARELESS. Your uncle Oliver! Gad, then you'll never be friends, Charles. That, now, to me, is as stern a looking rogue as ever I saw; an unforgiving eye, and a damned disinheriting countenance! an inveterate knave, depend on't. Don't you think so, little Premium?

SIR OLIVER. Upon my soul, Sir, I do not; I think it is as honest a looking face as any in the room, dead or alive. But I suppose uncle Oliver goes with the rest of the lumber?

CHARLES. No, hang it! I'll not part with poor Noll. The old fellow has been very good to me, and, egad, I'll keep his picture while I've a room to put it in.

SIR OLIVER. [Aside.] The rogue's my nephew after all!---[Aloud.] But, sir, I have somehow taken a fancy to that picture.

CHARLES. I'm sorry for't, for you certainly will not have it. Oons, haven't you got enough of

53

them?

SIR OLIVER. [Aside.] I forgive him everything!---[Aloud.] But, Sir, when I take a whim in my head, I don't value money. I'll give you as much for that as for all the rest.

CHARLES. Don't tease me, master broker; I tell you I'll not part with it, and there's an end of it.

SIR OLIVER. [Aside.] How like his father the dog is.---[Aloud.] Well, well, I have done.--- [Aside.] I did not perceive it before, but I think I never saw such a striking resemblance.--- [Aloud.] Here is a draught for your sum.

CHARLES. Why, 'tis for eight hundred pounds!

SIR OLIVER. You will not let Sir Oliver go?

CHARLES. Zounds! no! I tell you, once more.

SIR OLIVER. Then never mind the difference, we'll balance that another time. But give me your hand on the bargain; you are an honest fellow, Charles---I beg pardon, sir, for being so free.--- Come, Moses.

CHARLES. Egad, this is a whimsical old fellow!---But hark'ee, Premium, you'll prepare lodgings for these gentlemen.

SIR OLIVER. Yes, yes, I'll send for them in a day or two.

CHARLES. But, hold; do now send a genteel conveyance for them, for, I assure you, they were most of them used to ride in their own carriages.

SIR OLIVER. I will, I will---for all but Oliver.

CHARLES. Ay, all but the little nabob.

SIR OLIVER. You're fixed on that?

CHARLES. Peremptorily.

SIR OLIVER. [Aside.] A dear extravagant rogue!---[Aloud.] Good day! Come, Moses.---[Aside.] Let me hear now who dares call him profligate!

CARELESS. Why, this is the oddest genius of the sort I ever met with!

CHARLES. Egad, he's the prince of brokers, I think. I wonder how the devil Moses got acquainted with so honest a fellow.---Ha! here's Rowley.---Do, Careless, say I'll join the company in a few moments.

CARELESS. I will---but don't let that old blockhead persuade you to squander any of that money on old musty debts, or any such nonsense; for tradesmen, Charles, are the most exorbitant fellows.

CHARLES. Very true, and paying them is only encouraging them.

CARELESS. Nothing else.

CHARLES. Ay, ay, never fear.---

[Exit CARELESS.]

So! this was an odd old fellow, indeed. Let me see, two-thirds of these five hundred and thirty odd pounds are mine by right. Fore Heaven! I find one's ancestors are more valuable relations than I took them for!---Ladies and gentlemen, your most obedient and very grateful servant.   [Bows ceremoniously to the pictures.]

    Enter ROWLEY

Ha! old Rowley! egad, you are just come in time to take leave of your old acquaintance.

ROWLEY. Yes, I heard they were a-going. But I wonder you can have such spirits under so many distresses.

CHARLES. Why, there's the point! my distresses are so many, that I can't affort to part with my spirits; but I shall be rich and splenetic, all in good time. However, I suppose you are surprised that I am not more sorrowful at parting with so many near relations; to be sure, 'tis very affecting; but you see they never move a muscle, so why should I?

ROWLEY. There's no making you serious a moment.

CHARLES. Yes, faith, I am so now. Here, my honest Rowley, here, get me this changed directly, and take a hundred pounds of it immediately to old Stanley.

ROWLEY. A hundred pounds! Consider only------

CHARLES. Gad's life, don't talk about it! poor Stanley's wants are pressing, and, if you don't make haste, we shall have some one call that has a better right to the money.

ROWLEY. Ah! there's the point! I never will cease dunning you with the old proverb------

CHARLES. BE JUST BEFORE YOU'RE GENEROUS.---Why, so I would if I could; but Justice is an old hobbling beldame, and I can't get her to keep pace with Generosity, for the soul of me.

ROWLEY. Yet, Charles, believe me, one hour's reflection------

CHARLES. Ay, ay, it's very true; but, hark'ee, Rowley, while I have, by Heaven I'll give; so, damn your economy! and now for hazard.

[Exeunt.]

SCENE II.---The Parlour

Enter SIR OLIVER and MOSES

MOSES. Well sir, I think as Sir Peter said you have seen Mr. Charles in high Glory---'tis great Pity He's so extravagant.

SIR OLIVER. True---but he would not sell my Picture---

MOSES. And loves wine and women so much---

SIR OLIVER. But He wouldn't sell my Picture.

MOSES. And game so deep---

SIR OLIVER. But He wouldn't sell my Picture. O---here's Rowley!

Enter ROWLEY

ROWLEY. So---Sir Oliver---I find you have made a Purchase------

SIR OLIVER. Yes---yes---our young Rake has parted with his Ancestors like old Tapestry---sold Judges and Generals by the foot---and maiden Aunts as cheap as broken China.---

ROWLEY. And here has he commissioned me to re-deliver you Part of the purchase-money---I mean tho' in your necessitous character of old Stanley------

MOSES. Ah! there is the Pity of all! He is so damned charitable.

ROWLEY. And I left a Hosier and two Tailors in the Hall---who I'm sure won't be paid, and this hundred would satisfy 'em.

SIR OLIVER. Well---well---I'll pay his debts and his Benevolences too---I'll take care of old Stanley---myself---But now I am no more a Broker, and you shall introduce me to the elder Brother as Stanley------

ROWLEY. Not yet a while---Sir Peter I know means to call there about this time.

Enter TRIP

TRIP. O Gentlemen---I beg Pardon for not showing you out---this way---Moses, a word.

[Exit TRIP with MOSES.]

SIR OLIVER. There's a Fellow for you---Would you believe it that Puppy intercepted the Jew, on our coming, and wanted to raise money before he got to his master!

ROWLEY. Indeed!

SIR OLIVER. Yes---they are now planning an annuity Business---Ah Master Rowley[,] in my Day Servants were content with the Follies of their Masters when they were worn a little Thread Bare but now they have their Vices like their Birth Day cloaths with the gloss on.

[Exeunt.]

SCENE III.---A Library

SURFACE. No letter from Lady Teazle?

SERVANT. No Sir---

SURFACE. I am surprised she hasn't sent if she is prevented from coming---! Sir Peter certainly does not suspect me---yet I wish I may not lose the Heiress, thro' the scrape I have drawn myself in with the wife---However, Charles's imprudence and bad character are great Points in my Favour.

SERVANT. Sir---I believe that must be Lady Teazle---

SURFACE. Hold[!] see---whether it is or not before you go to the Door---I have a particular Message for you if it should be my Brother.

SERVANT. 'Tis her ladyship Sir---She always leaves her Chair at the milliner's in the next Street.

SURFACE. Stay---stay---draw that Screen before the Window---that will do---my opposite Neighbour is a maiden Lady of so curious a temper!---

[SERVANT draws the screen and exit.]

I have a difficult Hand to play in this Affair---Lady Teazle as lately suspected my Views on Maria---but She must by no means be let into that secret, at least till I have her more in my Power.

Enter LADY TEAZLE

LADY TEAZLE. What[!] Sentiment in soliloquy---have you been very impatient now?---O Lud! don't pretend to look grave---I vow I couldn't come before------

SURFACE. O Madam[,] Punctuality is a species of Constancy, a very unfashionable quality in a Lady.

LADY TEAZLE. Upon my word you ought to pity me, do you now Sir Peter is grown so ill-tempered to me of Late! and so jealous! of Charles too that's the best of the story isn't it?

SURFACE. I am glad my scandalous Friends keep that up. [Aside.]

LADY TEAZLE. I am sure I wish He would let Maria marry him---and then perhaps He would be convinced---don't you---Mr. Surface?

SURFACE. Indeed I do not.---[Aside.] O certainly I do---for then my dear Lady Teazle would also be convinced how wrong her suspicions were of my having any design on the silly Girl------

LADY TEAZLE. Well---well I'm inclined to believe you---besides I really never could perceive why she should have so any admirers.

SURFACE. O for her Fortune---nothing else---

LADY TEAZLE. I believe so for tho' she is certainly very pretty---yet she has no conversation in the world---and is so grave and reserved---that I declare I think she'd have made an excellent wife for Sir Peter.---

SURFACE. So she would.

LADY TEAZLE. Then---one never hears her speak ill of anybody---which you know is mighty dull---

SURFACE. Yet she doesn't want understanding---

LADY TEAZLE. No more she does---yet one is always disapointed when one hears [her] speak---For though her Eyes have no kind of meaning in them---she very seldom talks Nonsense.

SURFACE. Nay---nay surely---she has very fine eyes---

LADY TEAZLE. Why so she has---tho' sometimes one fancies there's a little sort of a squint---

SURFACE. A squint---O fie---Lady Teazle.

LADY TEAZLE. Yes yes---I vow now---come there is a left-handed Cupid in one eye---that's the Truth on't.

SURFACE. Well---his aim is very direct however---but Lady Sneerwell has quite corrupted you.

LADY TEAZLE. No indeed---I have not opinion enough of her to be taught by her, and I know that she has lately rais'd many scandalous hints of me---which you know one always hears from one common Friend, or other.

SURFACE. Why to say truth I believe you are not more obliged to her than others of her acquaintance.

LADY TEAZLE. But isn't [it] provoking to hear the most ill-natured Things said to one and there's my friend Lady Sneerwell has circulated I don't know how many scandalous tales of me, and all without any foundation, too; that's what vexes me.

SURFACE. Aye Madam to be sure that is the Provoking circumstance---without Foundation---yes yes---there's the mortification indeed---for when a slanderous story is believed against one---there certainly is no comfort like the consciousness of having deserved it------

LADY TEAZLE. No to be sure---then I'd forgive their malice---but to attack me, who am really so innocent---and who never say an ill-natured thing of anybody---that is, of any Friend---! and then Sir Peter too---to have him so peevish---and so suspicious---when I know the integrity of my own Heart---indeed 'tis monstrous.

SURFACE. But my dear Lady Teazle 'tis your own fault if you suffer it---when a Husband entertains a groundless suspicion of his Wife and withdraws his confidence from her---the original compact is broke and she owes it to the Honour of her sex to endeavour to outwit him---

LADY TEAZLE. Indeed---So that if He suspects me without cause it follows that the best way of curing his jealousy is to give him reason for't---

SURFACE. Undoubtedly---for your Husband [should] never be deceived in you---and in that case it becomes you to be frail in compliment to his discernment---

LADY TEAZLE. To be sure what you say is very reasonable---and when the consciousness of my own Innocence------

SURFACE. Ah: my dear---Madam there is the great mistake---'tis this very conscious Innocence that is of the greatest Prejudice to you---what is it makes you negligent of Forms and careless of the world's opinion---why the consciousness of your Innocence---what makes you thoughtless in your Conduct and apt to run into a thousand little imprudences---why the consciousness of your Innocence---what makes you impatient of Sir Peter's temper, and outrageous at his suspicions--- why the consciousness of your own Innocence---

LADY TEAZLE. 'Tis very true.

SURFACE. Now my dear Lady Teazle if you but once make a trifling Faux Pas you can't conceive how cautious you would grow, and how ready to humour and agree with your Husband.

LADY TEAZLE. Do you think so---

SURFACE. O I'm sure on't; and then you'd find all scandal would cease at once---for in short your Character at Present is like a Person in a Plethora, absolutely dying of too much Health---

LADY TEAZLE. So---so---then I perceive your Prescription is that I must sin in my own Defence---and part with my virtue to preserve my Reputation.---

SURFACE. Exactly so upon my credit Ma'am[.]

LADY TEAZLE. Well certainly this is the oddest Doctrine---and the newest Receipt for avoiding calumny.

SURFACE. An infallible one believe me---Prudence like experience must be paid for---

LADY TEAZLE. Why if my understanding were once convinced------

SURFACE. Oh, certainly Madam, your understanding SHOULD be convinced---yes---yes---Heaven forbid I should persuade you to do anything you THOUGHT wrong---no---no---I have too much honor to desire it---

LADY TEAZLE. Don't---you think we may as well leave Honor out of the Argument? [Rises.]

SURFACE. Ah---the ill effects of your country education I see still remain with you.

LADY TEAZLE. I doubt they do indeed---and I will fairly own to you, that If I could be persuaded to do wrong it would be by Sir Peter's ill-usage---sooner than your honourable Logic, after all.

SURFACE. Then by this Hand, which He is unworthy of------

Enter SERVANT

Sdeath, you Blockhead---what do you want?

SERVANT. I beg your Pardon Sir, but I thought you wouldn't chuse Sir Peter to come up without announcing him?

SURFACE. Sir Peter---Oons---the Devil!

LADY TEAZLE. Sir Peter! O Lud! I'm ruined! I'm ruin'd!

SERVANT. Sir, 'twasn't I let him in.

LADY TEAZLE. O I'm undone---what will become of me now Mr. Logick.---Oh! mercy, He's on the Stairs---I'll get behind here---and if ever I'm so imprudent again------

[Goes behind the screen---]

SURFACE. Give me that---Book!------

[Sits down---SERVANT pretends to adjust his Hair---]

Enter SIR PETER

SIR PETER. Aye---ever improving himself!---Mr. Surface---

SURFACE. Oh! my dear Sir Peter---I beg your Pardon---[Gaping and throws away the Book.] I have been dosing [dozing] over a stupid Book! well---I am much obliged to you for this Call---You haven't been here I believe since I fitted up this Room---Books you know are the only Things I am a Coxcomb in---

SIR PETER. 'Tis very neat indeed---well well that's proper---and you make even your Screen a source of knowledge---hung I perceive with Maps---

SURFACE. O yes---I find great use in that Screen.

SIR PETER. I dare say you must---certainly---when you want to find out anything in a Hurry.

SURFACE. Aye or to hide anything in a Hurry either---

SIR PETER. Well I have a little private Business---if we were alone---

SURFACE. You needn't stay.

SERVANT. No---Sir------

[Exit SERVANT.]

SURFACE. Here's a Chair---Sir Peter---I beg------

SIR PETER. Well---now we are alone---there IS a subject---my dear Friend---on which I wish to unburthen my Mind to you---a Point of the greatest moment to my Peace---in short, my good Friend---Lady Teazle's conduct of late has made me very unhappy.

SURFACE. Indeed I'm very sorry to hear it---

SIR PETER. Yes 'tis but too plain she has not the least regard for me---but what's worse, I have pretty good Authority to suspect that she must have formed an attachment to another.

SURFACE. Indeed! you astonish me.

SIR PETER. Yes---and between ourselves---I think I have discover'd the Person.

SURFACE. How---you alarm me exceedingly!

SIR PETER. Ah: my dear Friend I knew you would sympathize with me.---

SURFACE. Yes---believe me Sir Peter---such a discovery would hurt me just as much as it would you---

SIR PETER. I am convinced of it---ah---it is a happiness to have a Friend whom one can trust even with one's Family secrets---but have you no guess who I mean?

SURFACE. I haven't the most distant Idea---it can't be Sir Benjamin Backbite.

SIR PETER. O---No. What say you to Charles?

SURFACE. My Brother---impossible!---O no Sir Peter you mustn't credit the scandalous insinuations you hear---no no---Charles to be sure has been charged with many things but go I can never think He would meditate so gross an injury---

SIR PETER. Ah! my dear Friend---the goodness of your own Heart misleads you---you judge of others by yourself.

SURFACE. Certainly Sir Peter---the Heart that is conscious of its own integrity is ever slowest to credit another's Treachery.---

SIR PETER. True---but your Brother has no sentiment[---]you never hear him talk so.---

SURFACE. Well there certainly is no knowing what men are capable of---no---there is no knowing---yet I can't but think Lady Teazle herself has too much Principle------

SIR PETER. Aye but what's Principle against the Flattery of a handsome---lively young Fellow---

SURFACE. That's very true---

SIR PETER. And then you know the difference of our ages makes it very improbable that she should have any great affection for me---and if she were to be frail and I were to make it Public--- why the Town would only laugh at the foolish old Batchelor, who had married a girl------

SURFACE. That's true---to be sure People would laugh.

SIR PETER. Laugh---aye and make Ballads---and Paragraphs and the Devil knows what of me---

SURFACE. No---you must never make it public---

SIR PETER. But then again that the Nephew of my old Friend, Sir Oliver[,] should be the Person to attempt such an injury---hurts me more nearly---

SURFACE. Undoubtedly---when Ingratitude barbs the Dart of Injury---the wound has double danger in it---

SIR PETER. Aye---I that was in a manner left his Guardian---in his House he had been so often entertain'd---who never in my Life denied him my advice---

SURFACE. O 'tis not to be credited---There may be a man capable of such Baseness, to be sure--- but for my Part till you can give me positive Proofs you must excuse me withholding my Belief. However, if this should be proved on him He is no longer a brother of mine I disclaim kindred with him---for the man who can break thro' the Laws of Hospitality---and attempt the wife of his Friend deserves to be branded as the Pest of Society.

SIR PETER. What a difference there is between you---what noble sentiments!---

SURFACE. But I cannot suspect Lady Teazle's honor.

SIR PETER. I'm sure I wish to think well of her---and to remove all ground of Quarrel between us---She has lately reproach'd me more than once with having made no settlement on her---and, in our last Quarrel, she almost hinted that she should not break her Heart if I was dead.---now as we seem to differ in our Ideas of Expense I have resolved she shall be her own Mistress in that Respect for the future---and if I were to die---she shall find that I have not been inattentive to her Interests while living---Here my Friend are the Draughts of two Deeds which I wish to have your opinion on---by one she will enjoy eight hundred a year independent while I live---and by the other the bulk of my Fortune after my Death.

SURFACE. This conduct Sir Peter is indeed truly Generous! I wish it may not corrupt my pupil.---[Aside.]

SIR PETER. Yes I am determined she shall have no cause to complain---tho' I would not have her acquainted with the latter instance of my affection yet awhile.

SURFACE. Nor I---if I could help it.

SIR PETER. And now my dear Friend if you please we will talk over the situation of your Hopes with Maria.

SURFACE. No---no---Sir Peter---another Time if you Please---[softly].

SIR PETER. I am sensibly chagrined at the little Progress you seem to make in her affection.

SURFACE. I beg you will not mention it---What are my Disappointments when your Happiness is in Debate [softly]. 'Sdeath I shall be ruined every way.

SIR PETER. And tho' you are so averse to my acquainting Lady Teazle with YOUR passion, I am sure she's not your Enemy in the Affair.

SURFACE. Pray Sir Peter, now oblige me.---I am really too much affected by the subject we have been speaking of to bestow a thought on my own concerns---The Man who is entrusted with his Friend's Distresses can never------

Enter SERVANT

Well, Sir?

SERVANT. Your Brother Sir, is---speaking to a Gentleman in the Street, and says He knows you're within.

SURFACE. 'Sdeath, Blockhead---I'm NOT within---I'm out for the Day.

SIR PETER. Stay---hold---a thought has struck me---you shall be at home.

SURFACE. Well---well---let him up.---

[Exit SERVANT.]

He'll interrupt Sir Peter, however. [Aside.]

SIR PETER. Now, my good Friend---oblige me I Intreat you---before Charles comes---let me conceal myself somewhere---Then do you tax him on the Point we have been talking on---and his answers may satisfy me at once.---

SURFACE. O Fie---Sir Peter---would you have ME join in so mean a Trick? to trepan my Brother too?

SIR PETER. Nay you tell me you are SURE He is innocent---if so you do him the greatest service in giving him an opportunity to clear himself---and---you will set my Heart at rest---come you shall not refuse me---here behind this Screen will be---hey! what the Devil---there seems to be one listener here already---I'll swear I saw a Petticoat.---

SURFACE. Ha! ha! ha! Well this is ridiculous enough---I'll tell you, Sir Peter---tho' I hold a man of Intrigue to be a most despicable Character---yet you know it doesn't follow that a man is to be an absolute Joseph either---hark'ee---'tis a little French Milliner---a silly Rogue that plagues me--- and having some character, on your coming she ran behind the Screen.---

SIR PETER. Ah a Rogue---but 'egad she has overheard all I have been saying of my Wife.

SURFACE. O 'twill never go any farther, you may depend on't.

SIR PETER. No!---then efaith let her hear it out.---Here's a Closet will do as well.---

SURFACE. Well, go in there.---

SIR PETER. Sly rogue---sly Rogue.---

SURFACE. Gad's my Life what an Escape---! and a curious situation I'm in!---to part man and wife in this manner.---

LADY TEAZLE. [peeps out.] Couldn't I steal off---

SURFACE. Keep close, my Angel!

SIR PETER. [Peeping out.] Joseph---tax him home.

SURFACE. Back---my dear Friend

LADY TEAZLE. [Peeping out.] Couldn't you lock Sir Peter in?---

SURFACE. Be still---my Life!

SIR PETER. [Peeping.] You're sure the little Milliner won't blab?

SURFACE. In! in! my good Sir Peter---'Fore Gad, I wish I had a key to the Door.

Enter CHARLES

CHARLES. Hollo! Brother---what has been the matter? your Fellow wouldn't let me up at first---What[?] have you had a Jew or a wench with you.---

SURFACE. Neither Brother I assure you.

CHARLES. But---what has made Sir Peter steal off---I thought He had been with you---

SURFACE. He WAS Brother---but hearing you were coming He didn't chuse to stay---

CHARLES. What[!] was the old Gentleman afraid I wanted to borrow money of him?

SURFACE. No Sir---but I am sorry to find[,] Charles---you have lately given that worthy man grounds for great Uneasiness.

CHARLES. Yes they tell me I do that to a great many worthy men---but how so Pray?

SURFACE. To be plain with you Brother He thinks you are endeavouring to gain Lady Teazle's Affections from him.

CHARLES. Who I---O Lud! not I upon my word.---Ha! ha! ha! so the old Fellow has found out that He has got a young wife has He? or what's worse she has discover'd that she has an old Husband?

SURFACE. This is no subject to jest on Brother---He who can laugh------

CHARLES. True true as you were going to say---then seriously I never had the least idea of what you charge me with, upon my honour.

SURFACE. Well it will give Sir Peter great satisfaction to hear this.

CHARLES. [Aloud.] To be sure, I once thought the lady seemed to have taken a fancy---but upon my soul I never gave her the least encouragement.---Beside you know my Attachment to Maria---

SURFACE. But sure Brother even if Lady Teazle had betray'd the fondest Partiality for you------

CHARLES. Why---look'ee Joseph---I hope I shall never deliberately do a dishonourable Action---but if a pretty woman was purposely to throw herself in my way---and that pretty woman married to a man old enough to be her Father------

SURFACE. Well?

CHARLES. Why I believe I should be obliged to borrow a little of your Morality, that's all.---but, Brother do you know now that you surprize me exceedingly by naming me with Lady Teazle---for faith I always understood YOU were her Favourite---

SURFACE. O for shame---Charles---This retort is Foolish.

CHARLES. Nay I swear I have seen you exchange such significant Glances------

SURFACE. Nay---nay---Sir---this is no jest---

CHARLES. Egad---I'm serious---Don't you remember---one Day, when I called here------

SURFACE. Nay---prithee---Charles

CHARLES. And found you together------

SURFACE. Zounds, Sir---I insist------

CHARLES. And another time when your Servant------

SURFACE. Brother---brother a word with you---Gad I must stop him---[Aside.]

CHARLES. Informed---me that------

SURFACE. Hush!---I beg your Pardon but Sir Peter has overheard all we have been saying---I knew you would clear yourself, or I shouldn't have consented---

CHARLES. How Sir Peter---Where is He---

SURFACE. Softly, there! [Points to the closet.]

CHARLES. [In the Closet!] O 'fore Heaven I'll have him out---Sir Peter come forth!

SURFACE. No---no------

CHARLES. I say Sir Peter---come into court.---

[Pulls in SIR PETER.]

What---my old Guardian---what[!] turn inquisitor and take evidence incog.---

SIR PETER. Give me your hand---Charles---I believe I have suspected you wrongfully; but you mustn't be angry with Joseph---'twas my Plan---

CHARLES. Indeed!---

SIR PETER. But I acquit you---I promise you I don't think near so ill of you as I did---what I have heard has given me great satisfaction.

CHARLES. Egad then 'twas lucky you didn't hear any more. Wasn't it Joseph?

SIR PETER. Ah! you would have retorted on him.

CHARLES. Aye---aye---that was a Joke.

SIR PETER. Yes, yes, I know his honor too well.

CHARLES. Yet you might as well have suspected him as me in this matter, for all that---mightn't He, Joseph?

SIR PETER. Well well I believe you---

SURFACE. Would they were both out of the Room!

Enter SERVANT, whispers SURFACE

SIR PETER. And in future perhaps we may not be such Strangers.

SURFACE. Gentlemen---I beg Pardon---I must wait on you downstairs---Here is a Person come on particular Business------

CHARLES. Well you can see him in another Room---Sir Peter and I haven't met a long time and I have something to say [to] him.

SURFACE. They must not be left together.---I'll send this man away and return directly---

[SURFACE goes out.]

SIR PETER. Ah---Charles if you associated more with your Brother, one might indeed hope for your reformation---He is a man of Sentiment---Well! there is nothing in the world so noble as a man of Sentiment!

CHARLES. Pshaw! He is too moral by half---and so apprehensive of his good Name, as he calls it, that I suppose He would as soon let a Priest in his House as a Girl---

SIR PETER. No---no---come come,---you wrong him. No, no, Joseph is no Rake but he is no such Saint in that respect either. I have a great mind to tell him---we should have such a Laugh!

CHARLES. Oh, hang him? He's a very Anchorite---a young Hermit!

SIR PETER. Harkee---you must not abuse him, he may chance to hear of it again I promise you.

CHARLES. Why you won't tell him?

SIR PETER. No---but---this way. Egad, I'll tell him---Harkee, have you a mind to have a good laugh against Joseph?

CHARLES. I should like it of all things---

SIR PETER. Then, E'faith, we will---I'll be quit with him for discovering me.---He had a girl with him when I called. [Whispers.]

CHARLES. What[!] Joseph[!] you jest---

SIR PETER. Hush!---a little French Milliner---and the best of the jest is---she's in the room now.

CHARLES. The devil she is---

SIR PETER. Hush! I tell you. [Points.]

CHARLES. Behind the screen! Odds Life, let's unveil her!

SIR PETER. No---no! He's coming---you shan't indeed!

CHARLES. Oh, egad, we'll have a peep at the little milliner!

SIR PETER. Not for the world---Joseph will never forgive me.

CHARLES. I'll stand by you------

SIR PETER. Odds Life! Here He's coming---

[SURFACE enters just as CHARLES throws down the Screen.]

Re-enter JOSEPH SURFACE

CHARLES. Lady Teazle! by all that's wonderful!

SIR PETER. Lady Teazle! by all that's Horrible!

CHARLES. Sir Peter---This is one of the smartest French Milliners I ever saw!---Egad, you seem all to have been diverting yourselves here at Hide and Seek---and I don't see who is out of the Secret!---Shall I beg your Ladyship to inform me!---Not a word!---Brother!---will you please to explain this matter? What! is Honesty Dumb too?---Sir Peter, though I found you in the Dark---perhaps you are not so now---all mute! Well tho' I can make nothing of the Affair, I make no doubt but you perfectly understand one another---so I'll leave you to yourselves.---[Going.] Brother I'm sorry to find you have given that worthy man grounds for so much uneasiness!---Sir Peter---there's nothing in the world so noble as a man of Sentiment!---

[Stand for some time looking at one another. Exit CHARLES.]

SURFACE. Sir Peter---notwithstanding I confess that appearances are against me. If you will afford me your Patience I make no doubt but I shall explain everything to your satisfaction.---

SIR PETER. If you please---Sir---

SURFACE. The Fact is Sir---that Lady Teazle knowing my Pretensions to your ward Maria---I say Sir Lady Teazle---being apprehensive of the Jealousy of your Temper---and knowing my Friendship to the Family. S he Sir---I say call'd here---in order that I might explain those Pretensions---but on your coming being apprehensive---as I said of your Jealousy---she withdrew---and this, you may depend on't is the whole truth of the Matter.

SIR PETER. A very clear account upon the [my] word and I dare swear the Lady will vouch for every article of it.

LADY TEAZLE. For not one word of it Sir Peter---

SIR PETER. How[!] don't you think it worthwhile to agree in the lie.

65

LADY TEAZLE. There is not one Syllable of Truth in what that Gentleman has told you.

SIR PETER. I believe you upon my soul Ma'am---

SURFACE. 'Sdeath, madam, will you betray me! [Aside.]

LADY TEAZLE. Good Mr. Hypocrite by your leave I will speak for myself---

SIR PETER. Aye let her alone Sir---you'll find she'll make out a better story than you without Prompting.

LADY TEAZLE. Hear me Sir Peter---I came hither on no matter relating to your ward and even ignorant of this Gentleman's pretensions to her---but I came---seduced by his insidious arguments---and pretended Passion[---]at least to listen to his dishonourable Love if not to sacrifice your Honour to his Baseness.

SIR PETER. Now, I believe, the Truth is coming indeed[.]

SURFACE. The Woman's mad---

LADY TEAZLE. No Sir---she has recovered her Senses. Your own Arts have furnished her with the means. Sir Peter---I do not expect you to credit me---but the Tenderness you express'd for me, when I am sure you could not think I was a witness to it, has penetrated so to my Heart that had I left the Place without the Shame of this discovery---my future life should have spoken the sincerity of my Gratitude---as for that smooth-tongued Hypocrite---who would have seduced the wife of his too credulous Friend while he pretended honourable addresses to his ward---I behold him now in a light so truly despicable that I shall never again Respect myself for having Listened to him.
[Exit.]

SURFACE. Notwithstanding all this Sir Peter---Heaven knows------

SIR PETER. That you are a Villain!---and so I leave you to your conscience---

SURFACE. You are too Rash Sir Peter---you SHALL hear me---The man who shuts out conviction by refusing to------
[Exeunt, SURFACE following and speaking.]

END OF THE FOURTH

ACT V

SCENE I.---The Library

SURFACE. Mr. Stanley! and why should you think I would see him?---you must know he came to ask something!

SERVANT. Sir---I shouldn't have let him in but that Mr. Rowley came to the Door with him.

SURFACE. Pshaw!---Blockhead to suppose that I should now be in a Temper to receive visits from poor Relations!---well why don't you show the Fellow up?

SERVANT. I will---Sir---Why, Sir---it was not my Fault that Sir Peter discover'd my Lady------

SURFACE. Go, fool!---

[Exit SERVANT.]

Sure Fortune never play'd a man of my policy such a Trick before---my character with Sir Peter!---my Hopes with Maria!---destroy'd in a moment!---I'm in a rare Humour to listen to other People's Distresses!---I shan't be able to bestow even a benevolent sentiment on Stanley---So! here---He comes and Rowley with him---I MUST try to recover myself, and put a little Charity into my Face however.------

[Exit.]

Enter SIR OLIVER and ROWLEY

SIR OLIVER. What! does He avoid us? that was He---was it not?

ROWLEY. It was Sir---but I doubt you are come a little too abruptly---his Nerves are so weak that the sight of a poor Relation may be too much for him---I should have gone first to break you to him.

SIR OLIVER. A Plague of his Nerves---yet this is He whom Sir Peter extolls as a Man of the most Benevolent way of thinking!---

ROWLEY. As to his way of thinking---I can't pretend to decide[,] for, to do him justice He appears to have as much speculative Benevolence as any private Gentleman in the Kingdom---though he is seldom so sensual as to indulge himself in the exercise of it------

SIR OLIVER. Yet [he] has a string of charitable Sentiments I suppose at his Fingers' ends!---

ROWLEY. Or, rather at his Tongue's end Sir Oliver; for I believe there is no sentiment he has more faith in than that 'Charity begins at Home.'

SIR OLIVER. And his I presume is of that domestic sort which never stirs abroad at all.

ROWLEY. I doubt you'll find it so---but He's coming---I mustn't seem to interrupt you---and you know immediately---as you leave him---I come in to announce---your arrival in your real Character.

SIR OLIVER. True---and afterwards you'll meet me at Sir Peter's------

ROWLEY. Without losing a moment.

[Exit.]

SIR OLIVER. So---I see he has premeditated a Denial by the Complaisance of his Features.

Enter SURFACE

SURFACE. Sir---I beg you ten thousand Pardons for keeping---you a moment waiting---Mr. Stanley---I presume------

SIR OLIVER. At your Service.

SURFACE. Sir---I beg you will do me the honour to sit down---I entreat you Sir.

SIR OLIVER. Dear Sir there's no occasion---too civil by half!

SURFACE. I have not the Pleasure of knowing you, Mr. Stanley---but I am extremely happy to see you look so well---you were nearly related to my mother---I think Mr. Stanley------

SIR OLIVER. I was Sir---so nearly that my present Poverty I fear may do discredit to her Wealthy Children---else I should not have presumed to trouble you.---

SURFACE. Dear Sir---there needs no apology---He that is in Distress tho' a stranger has a right to claim kindred with the wealthy---I am sure I wish I was of that class, and had it in my power to offer you even a small relief.

SIR OLIVER. If your Unkle, Sir Oliver were here---I should have a Friend------

SURFACE. I wish He was Sir, with all my Heart---you should not want an advocate with him---believe me Sir.

SIR OLIVER. I should not need one---my Distresses would recommend me.---but I imagined---his Bounty had enabled you to become the agent of his Charity.

SURFACE. My dear Sir---you are strangely misinformed---Sir Oliver is a worthy Man, a worthy man---a very worthy sort of Man---but avarice Mr. Stanley is the vice of age---I will tell you my good Sir in confidence:---what he has done for me has been a mere---nothing[;] tho' People I know have thought otherwise and for my Part I never chose to contradict the Report.

SIR OLIVER. What!---has he never transmitted---you---Bullion---Rupees---Pagodas!

SURFACE. O Dear Sir---Nothing of the kind---no---no---a few Presents now and then---china, shawls, congo Tea, Avadavats---and indian Crackers---little more, believe me.

SIR OLIVER. Here's Gratitude for twelve thousand pounds!---Avadavats and indian Crackers.

SURFACE. Then my dear---Sir---you have heard, I doubt not, of the extravagance of my Brother---Sir---there are very few would credit what I have done for that unfortunate young man.

SIR OLIVER. Not I for one!

SURFACE. The sums I have lent him! indeed---I have been exceedingly to blame---it was an amiable weakness! however I don't pretend to defend it---and now I feel it doubly culpable---since it has deprived me of the power of serving YOU Mr. Stanley as my Heart directs------

SIR OLIVER. Dissembler! Then Sir---you cannot assist me?

SURFACE. At Present it grieves me to say I cannot---but whenever I have the ability, you may depend upon hearing from me.

SIR OLIVER. I am extremely sorry------

SURFACE. Not more than I am believe me---to pity without the Power to relieve is still more painful than to ask and be denied------

SIR OLIVER. Kind Sir---your most obedient humble servant.

SURFACE. You leave me deeply affected Mr. Stanley---William---be ready to open the door------

SIR OLIVER. O, Dear Sir, no ceremony------

SURFACE. Your very obedient------

SIR OLIVER. Your most obsequious------

SURFACE. You may depend on hearing from me whenever I can be of service------

SIR OLIVER. Sweet Sir---you are too good------

SURFACE. In the mean time I wish you Health and Spirits------

SIR OLIVER. Your ever grateful and perpetual humble Servant------

SURFACE. Sir---yours as sincerely------

SIR OLIVER. Charles!---you are my Heir.

[Exit.]

SURFACE, solus Soh!---This is one bad effect of a good Character---it invites applications from the unfortunate and there needs no small degree of address to gain the reputation of Benevolence without incurring the expence.---The silver ore of pure Charity is an expensive article in the catalogue of a man's good Qualities---whereas the sentimental French Plate I use instead of it makes just as good a shew---and pays no tax.

Enter ROWLEY

ROWLEY. Mr. Surface---your Servant: I was apprehensive of interrupting you, tho' my Business demands immediate attention---as this Note will inform you------

SURFACE. Always Happy to see Mr. Rowley---how---Oliver---Surface!---My Unkle arrived!

ROWLEY. He is indeed---we have just parted---quite well---after a speedy voyage---and impatient to embrace his worthy Nephew.

SURFACE. I am astonished!---William[!] stop Mr. Stanley, if He's not gone------

ROWLEY. O---He's out of reach---I believe.

SURFACE. Why didn't you let me know this when you came in together.---

ROWLEY. I thought you had particular---Business---but must be gone to inform your Brother, and appoint him here to meet his Uncle. He will be with you in a quarter of an hour------

SURFACE. So he says. Well---I am strangely overjoy'd at his coming---never to be sure was anything so damn'd unlucky!

ROWLEY. You will be delighted to see how well He looks.

SURFACE. O---I'm rejoiced to hear it---just at this time------

ROWLEY. I'll tell him how impatiently you expect him------

SURFACE. Do---do---pray---give my best duty and affection---indeed, I cannot express the sensations I feel at the thought of seeing him!---certainly his coming just at this Time is the cruellest piece of ill Fortune------

[Exeunt.]

SCENE II.---At SIR PETER'S House

Enter MRS. CANDOUR and SERVANT

SERVANT. Indeed Ma'am, my Lady will see nobody at Present.

MRS. CANDOUR. Did you tell her it was her Friend Mrs. Candour------

SERVANT. Yes Ma'am but she begs you will excuse her------

MRS. CANDOUR. Do go again---I shall be glad to see her if it be only for a moment---for I am sure she must be in great Distress

[exit MAID]

---Dear Heart---how provoking!---I'm not mistress of half the circumstances!---We shall have the whole affair in the newspapers with the Names of the Parties at length before I have dropt the story at a dozen houses.

Enter SIR BENJAMIN

Sir Benjamin you have heard, I suppose------

SIR BENJAMIN. Of Lady Teazle and Mr. Surface------

MRS. CANDOUR. And Sir Peter's Discovery------

SIR BENJAMIN. O the strangest Piece of Business to be sure------

MRS. CANDOUR. Well I never was so surprised in my life!---I am so sorry for all Parties---indeed,

SIR BENJAMIN. Now I don't Pity Sir Peter at all---he was so extravagant---partial to Mr. Surface------

MRS. CANDOUR. Mr. Surface!---why 'twas with Charles Lady Teazle was detected.

SIR BENJAMIN. No such thing Mr. Surface is the gallant.

MRS. CANDOUR. No---no---Charles is the man---'twas Mr. Surface brought Sir Peter on purpose to discover them------

SIR BENJAMIN. I tell you I have it from one------

MRS. CANDOUR. And I have it from one------

SIR BENJAMIN. Who had it from one who had it------

MRS. CANDOUR. From one immediately---but here comes Lady Sneerwell---perhaps she knows the whole affair.

Enter LADY SNEERWELL

LADY SNEERWELL. So---my dear Mrs. Candour Here's a sad affair of our Friend Teazle------

MRS. CANDOUR. Aye my dear Friend, who could have thought it.

LADY SNEERWELL. Well there is no trusting to appearances[;] tho'---indeed she was always too lively for me.

MRS. CANDOUR. To be sure, her manners were a little too---free---but she was very young------

LADY SNEERWELL. And had indeed some good Qualities.

MRS. CANDOUR. So she had indeed---but have you heard the Particulars?

LADY SNEERWELL. No---but everybody says that Mr. Surface------

SIR BENJAMIN. Aye there I told you---Mr. Surface was the Man.

MRS. CANDOUR. No---no---indeed the assignation was with Charles------

LADY SNEERWELL. With Charles!---You alarm me Mrs. Candour!

MRS. CANDOUR. Yes---yes He was the Lover---Mr. Surface---do him justice---was only the Informer.

SIR BENJAMIN. Well I'll not dispute with you Mrs. Candour---but be it which it may---I hope that Sir Peter's wound will not------

MRS. CANDOUR. Sir Peter's wound! O mercy! I didn't hear a word of their Fighting------

LADY SNEERWELL. Nor I a syllable!

SIR BENJAMIN. No---what no mention of the Duel------

MRS. CANDOUR. Not a word---

SIR BENJAMIN. O, Lord---yes---yes---they fought before they left the Room.

LADY SNEERWELL. Pray let us hear.

MRS. CANDOUR. Aye---do oblige---us with the Duel------

SIR BENJAMIN. 'Sir'---says Sir Peter---immediately after the Discovery, 'you are a most ungrateful Fellow.'

MRS. CANDOUR. Aye to Charles------

SIR BENJAMIN. No, no---to Mr. Surface---'a most ungrateful Fellow; and old as I am, Sir,' says He, 'I insist on immediate satisfaction.'

MRS. CANDOUR. Aye that must have been to Charles for 'tis very unlikely Mr. Surface should go to fight in his own House.

SIR BENJAMIN. Gad's Life, Ma'am, not at all---giving me immediate satisfaction---on this, Madam---Lady Teazle seeing Sir Peter in such Danger---ran out of the Room in strong Hysterics---and Charles after her calling out for Hartshorn and Water! Then Madam---they began to fight with Swords------

Enter CRABTREE

CRABTREE. With Pistols---Nephew---I have it from undoubted authority.

MRS. CANDOUR. Oh, Mr. Crabtree then it is all true------

CRABTREE. Too true indeed Ma'am, and Sir Peter Dangerously wounded------

SIR BENJAMIN. By a thrust in second---quite thro' his left side

CRABTREE. By a Bullet lodged in the Thorax------

MRS. CANDOUR. Mercy---on me[!] Poor Sir Peter------

CRABTREE. Yes, ma'am tho' Charles would have avoided the matter if he could------

MRS. CANDOUR. I knew Charles was the Person------

SIR BENJAMIN. O my Unkle I see knows nothing of the matter------

CRABTREE. But Sir Peter tax'd him with the basest ingratitude------

SIR BENJAMIN. That I told you, you know------

CRABTREE. Do Nephew let me speak---and insisted on immediate------

SIR BENJAMIN. Just as I said------

CRABTREE. Odds life! Nephew allow others to know something too---A Pair of Pistols lay on the Bureau---for Mr. Surface---it seems, had come home the Night before late from Salt-Hill where He had been to see the Montem with a Friend, who has a Son at Eton---so unluckily the Pistols were left Charged------

SIR BENJAMIN. I heard nothing of this------

CRABTREE. Sir Peter forced Charles to take one and they fired---it seems pretty nearly together---Charles's shot took Place as I tell you---and Sir Peter's miss'd---but what is very extraordinary the Ball struck against a little Bronze Pliny that stood over the Fire Place---grazed out of the window at a right angle---and wounded the Postman, who was just coming to the Door with a double letter from Northamptonshire.

SIR BENJAMIN. My Unkle's account is more circumstantial I must confess---but I believe mine is the true one for all that.

LADY SNEERWELL. I am more interested in this Affair than they imagine---and must have better information.---

[Exit.]

SIR BENJAMIN. Ah! Lady Sneerwell's alarm is very easily accounted for.---

CRABTREE. Yes yes, they certainly DO say---but that's neither here nor there.

MRS. CANDOUR. But pray where is Sir Peter at present------

CRABTREE. Oh! they---brought him home and He is now in the House, tho' the Servants are order'd to deny it------

MRS. CANDOUR. I believe so---and Lady Teazle---I suppose attending him------

CRABTREE. Yes yes---and I saw one of the Faculty enter just before me------

SIR BENJAMIN. Hey---who comes here------

CRABTREE. Oh, this is He---the Physician depend on't.

MRS. CANDOUR. O certainly it must be the Physician and now we shall know------

Enter SIR OLIVER

CRABTREE. Well, Doctor---what Hopes?

MRS. CANDOUR. Aye Doctor how's your Patient?

SIR BENJAMIN. Now Doctor isn't it a wound with a small sword------

CRABTREE. A bullet lodged in the Thorax---for a hundred!

SIR OLIVER. Doctor!---a wound with a small sword! and a Bullet in the Thorax!---oon's are you mad, good People?

SIR BENJAMIN. Perhaps, Sir, you are not a Doctor.

SIR OLIVER. Truly Sir I am to thank you for my degree If I am.

CRABTREE. Only a Friend of Sir Peter's then I presume---but, sir, you must have heard of this accident---

SIR OLIVER. Not a word!

CRABTREE. Not of his being dangerously wounded?

SIR OLIVER. The Devil he is!

SIR BENJAMIN. Run thro' the Body------

CRABTREE. Shot in the breast------

SIR BENJAMIN. By one Mr. Surface------

CRABTREE. Aye the younger.

SIR OLIVER. Hey! what the plague! you seem to differ strangely in your accounts---however you agree that Sir Peter is dangerously wounded.

SIR BENJAMIN. Oh yes, we agree in that.

CRABTREE. Yes, yes, I believe there can be no doubt in that.

SIR OLIVER. Then, upon my word, for a person in that Situation, he is the most imprudent man alive---For here he comes walking as if nothing at all was the matter.

Enter SIR PETER

Odd's heart, sir Peter! you are come in good time I promise you, for we had just given you over!

SIR BENJAMIN. 'Egad, Uncle this is the most sudden Recovery!

SIR OLIVER. Why, man, what do you do out of Bed with a Small Sword through your Body, and a Bullet lodg'd in your Thorax?

SIR PETER. A Small Sword and a Bullet---

SIR OLIVER. Aye these Gentlemen would have kill'd you without Law or Physic, and wanted to dub me a Doctor to make me an accomplice.

SIR PETER. Why! what is all this?

SIR BENJAMIN. We rejoice, Sir Peter, that the Story of the Duel is not true---and are sincerely sorry for your other Misfortune.

SIR PETER. So---so---all over the Town already! [Aside.]

CRABTREE. Tho', Sir Peter, you were certainly vastly to blame to marry at all at your years.

SIR PETER. Sir, what Business is that of yours?

MRS. CANDOUR. Tho' Indeed, as Sir Peter made so good a Husband, he's very much to be pitied.

SIR PETER. Plague on your pity, Ma'am, I desire none of it.

SIR BENJAMIN. However Sir Peter, you must not mind the Laughing and jests you will meet with on the occasion.

SIR PETER. Sir, I desire to be master in my own house.

CRABTREE. 'Tis no Uncommon Case, that's one comfort.

SIR PETER. I insist on being left to myself, without ceremony,---I insist on your leaving my house directly!

MRS. CANDOUR. Well, well, we are going and depend on't, we'll make the best report of you we can.

SIR PETER. Leave my house!

CRABTREE. And tell how hardly you have been treated.

SIR PETER. Leave my House---

SIR BENJAMIN. And how patiently you bear it.

SIR PETER. Friends! Vipers! Furies! Oh that their own Venom would choke them!

SIR OLIVER. They are very provoking indeed, Sir Peter.

Enter ROWLEY

ROWLEY. I heard high words: what has ruffled you Sir Peter---

SIR PETER. Pshaw what signifies asking---do I ever pass a Day without my Vexations?

SIR OLIVER. Well I'm not Inquisitive---I come only to tell you, that I have seen both my Nephews in the manner we proposed.

SIR PETER. A Precious Couple they are!

ROWLEY. Yes and Sir Oliver---is convinced that your judgment was right Sir Peter.

SIR OLIVER. Yes I find Joseph is Indeed the Man after all.

ROWLEY. Aye as Sir Peter says, He's a man of Sentiment.

SIR OLIVER. And acts up to the Sentiments he professes.

ROWLEY. It certainly is Edification to hear him talk.

SIR OLIVER. Oh, He's a model for the young men of the age! But how's this, Sir Peter? you don't Join us in your Friend Joseph's Praise as I expected.

SIR PETER. Sir Oliver, we live in a damned wicked world, and the fewer we praise the better.

ROWLEY. What do YOU say so, Sir Peter---who were never mistaken in your Life?

SIR PETER. Pshaw---Plague on you both---I see by your sneering you have heard---the whole affair---I shall go mad among you!

ROWLEY. Then to fret you no longer Sir Peter---we are indeed acquainted with it all---I met Lady Teazle coming from Mr. Surface's so humbled, that she deigned to request ME to be her advocate with you---

SIR PETER. And does Sir Oliver know all too?

SIR OLIVER. Every circumstance!

SIR PETER. What of the closet and the screen---hey[?]

SIR OLIVER. Yes yes---and the little French Milliner. Oh, I have been vastly diverted with the story! ha! ha! ha!

SIR PETER. 'Twas very pleasant!

SIR OLIVER. I never laugh'd more in my life, I assure you: ha! ha!

SIR PETER. O vastly diverting! ha! ha!

ROWLEY. To be sure Joseph with his Sentiments! ha! ha!

SIR PETER. Yes his sentiments! ha! ha! a hypocritical Villain!

SIR OLIVER. Aye and that Rogue Charles---to pull Sir Peter out of the closet: ha! ha!

SIR PETER. Ha! ha! 'twas devilish entertaining to be sure---

SIR OLIVER. Ha! ha! Egad, Sir Peter I should like to have seen your Face when the screen was thrown down---ha! ha!

SIR PETER. Yes, my face when the Screen was thrown down: ha! ha! ha! O I must never show my head again!

SIR OLIVER. But come---come it isn't fair to laugh at you neither my old Friend---tho' upon my soul I can't help it---

SIR PETER. O pray don't restrain your mirth on my account: it does not hurt me at all---I laugh at the whole affair myself---Yes---yes---I think being a standing Jest for all one's acquaintance a very happy situation---O yes---and then of a morning to read the Paragraphs about Mr. S------, Lady T------, and Sir P------, will be so entertaining!---I shall certainly leave town tomorrow and never look mankind in the Face again!

ROWLEY. Without affectation Sir Peter, you may despise the ridicule of Fools---but I see Lady Teazle going towards the next Room---I am sure you must desire a Reconciliation as earnestly as she does.

SIR OLIVER. Perhaps MY being here prevents her coming to you---well I'll leave honest Rowley to mediate between you; but he must bring you all presently to Mr. Surface's---where I am now returning---if not to reclaim a Libertine, at least to expose Hypocrisy.

SIR PETER. Ah! I'll be present at your discovering yourself there with all my heart; though 'tis a vile unlucky Place for discoveries.

SIR OLIVER. However it is very convenient to the carrying on of my Plot that you all live so near one another!

[Exit SIR OLIVER.]

ROWLEY. We'll follow---

SIR PETER. She is not coming here you see, Rowley---

ROWLEY. No but she has left the Door of that Room open you perceive.---see she is in Tears---!

SIR PETER. She seems indeed to wish I should go to her.---how dejected she appears---

ROWLEY. And will you refrain from comforting her---

SIR PETER. Certainly a little mortification appears very becoming in a wife---don't you think it will do her good to let her Pine a little.

ROWLEY. O this is ungenerous in you---

SIR PETER. Well I know not what to think---you remember Rowley the Letter I found of her's--- evidently intended for Charles?

ROWLEY. A mere forgery, Sir Peter---laid in your way on Purpose---this is one of the Points which I intend Snake shall give you conviction on---

SIR PETER. I wish I were once satisfied of that---She looks this way------what a remarkably elegant Turn of the Head she has! Rowley I'll go to her---

ROWLEY. Certainly---

SIR PETER. Tho' when it is known that we are reconciled, People will laugh at me ten times more!

ROWLEY. Let---them laugh---and retort their malice only by showing them you are happy in spite of it.

SIR PETER. Efaith so I will---and, if I'm not mistaken we may yet be the happiest couple in the country---

ROWLEY. Nay Sir Peter---He who once lays aside suspicion------

SIR PETER. Hold Master Rowley---if you have any Regard for me---never let me hear you utter anything like a Sentiment. I have had enough of THEM to serve me the rest of my Life.

[Exeunt.]

SCENE THE LAST.---The Library

SURFACE and LADY SNEERWELL

LADY SNEERWELL. Impossible! will not Sir Peter immediately be reconciled to CHARLES? and of consequence no longer oppose his union with MARIA? the thought is Distraction to me!

SURFACE. Can Passion---furnish a Remedy?

LADY SNEERWELL. No---nor cunning either. O I was a Fool, an Ideot---to league with such a Blunderer!

SURFACE. Surely Lady Sneerwell I am the greatest Sufferer---yet you see I bear the accident with Calmness.

LADY SNEERWELL. Because the Disappointment hasn't reached your HEART---your interest only attached you to Maria---had you felt for her---what I have for that ungrateful Libertine--- neither your Temper nor Hypocrisy could prevent your showing the sharpness of your Vexation.

SURFACE. But why should your Reproaches fall on me for this Disappointment?

LADY SNEERWELL. Are not you the cause of it? what had you to bate in your Pursuit of Maria to pervert Lady Teazle by the way.---had you not a sufficient field for your Roguery in blinding Sir Peter and supplanting your Brother---I hate such an avarice of crimes---'tis an unfair monopoly and never prospers.

SURFACE. Well I admit I have been to blame---I confess I deviated from the direct Road of wrong but I don't think we're so totally defeated neither.

LADY SNEERWELL. No!

SURFACE. You tell me you have made a trial of Snake since we met---and that you still believe him faithful to us---

LADY SNEERWELL. I do believe so.

SURFACE. And that he has undertaken should it be necessary---to swear and prove that Charles is at this Time contracted by vows and Honour to your Ladyship---which some of his former letters to you will serve to support---

LADY SNEERWELL. This, indeed, might have assisted---

SURFACE. Come---come it is not too late yet---but hark! this is probably my Unkle Sir Oliver--- retire to that Room---we'll consult further when He's gone.---

LADY SNEERWELL. Well but if HE should find you out to---

SURFACE. O I have no fear of that---Sir Peter will hold his tongue for his own credit sake---and you may depend on't I shall soon Discover Sir Oliver's weak side!---

LADY SNEERWELL. I have no diffidence of your abilities---only be constant to one roguery at a time---

[Exit.]

SURFACE. I will---I will---So 'tis confounded hard after such bad Fortune, to be baited by one's confederate in evil---well at all events my character is so much better than Charles's, that I certainly---hey---what!---this is not Sir Oliver---but old Stanley again!---Plague on't that He should return to teaze me just now---I shall have Sir Oliver come and find him here---and------

Enter SIR OLIVER

Gad's life, Mr. Stanley---why have you come back to plague me at this time? you must not stay now upon my word!

SIR OLIVER. Sir---I hear your Unkle Oliver is expected here---and tho' He has been so penurious to you, I'll try what He'll do for me---

SURFACE. Sir! 'tis impossible for you to stay now---so I must beg------come any other time and I promise you you shall be assisted.

SIR OLIVER. No---Sir Oliver and I must be acquainted---

SURFACE. Zounds Sir then [I] insist on your quitting the---Room directly---

SIR OLIVER. Nay Sir------

SURFACE. Sir---I insist on't---here William show this Gentleman out. Since you compel me Sir---not one moment---this is such insolence.
[Going to push him out.]

Enter CHARLES

CHARLES. Heyday! what's the matter now?---what the Devil have you got hold of my little Broker here! Zounds---Brother, don't hurt little Premium. What's the matter---my little Fellow?

SURFACE. So! He has been with you, too, has He---

CHARLES. To be sure He has! Why, 'tis as honest a little------But sure Joseph you have not been borrowing money too have you?

SURFACE. Borrowing---no!---But, Brother---you know sure we expect Sir Oliver every------

CHARLES. O Gad, that's true---Noll mustn't find the little Broker here to be sure---

SURFACE. Yet Mr. Stanley insists------

CHARLES. Stanley---why his name's Premium---

SURFACE. No no Stanley.

CHARLES. No, no---Premium.

SURFACE. Well no matter which---but------

CHARLES. Aye aye Stanley or Premium, 'tis the same thing as you say---for I suppose He goes by half a hundred Names, besides A. B's at the Coffee-House. [Knock.]

SURFACE. 'Sdeath---here's Sir Oliver at the Door------Now I beg---Mr. Stanley------

CHARLES. Aye aye and I beg Mr. Premium------

SIR OLIVER. Gentlemen------

SURFACE. Sir, by Heaven you shall go---

CHARLES. Aye out with him certainly------

SIR OLIVER. This violence------

SURFACE. 'Tis your own Fault.

CHARLES. Out with him to be sure. [Both forcing SIR OLIVER out.]

Enter SIR PETER TEAZLE, LADY TEAZLE, MARIA, and ROWLEY

SIR PETER. My old Friend, Sir Oliver!---hey! what in the name of wonder!---Here are dutiful Nephews!---assault their Unkle at his first Visit!

LADY TEAZLE. Indeed Sir Oliver 'twas well we came in to rescue you.

ROWLEY. Truly it was---for I perceive Sir Oliver the character of old Stanley was no Protection to you.

SIR OLIVER. Nor of Premium either---the necessities of the former could not extort a shilling from that benevolent Gentleman; and with the other I stood a chance of faring worse than my Ancestors, and being knocked down without being bid for.

SURFACE. Charles!

CHARLES. Joseph!

SURFACE. 'Tis compleat!

CHARLES. Very!

SIR OLIVER. Sir Peter---my Friend and Rowley too---look on that elder Nephew of mine---You know what He has already received from my Bounty and you know also how gladly I would have look'd on half my Fortune as held in trust for him---judge then my Disappointment in discovering him to be destitute of Truth---Charity---and Gratitude---

SIR PETER. Sir Oliver---I should be more surprized at this Declaration, if I had not myself found him to be selfish---treacherous and Hypocritical.

LADY TEAZLE. And if the Gentleman pleads not guilty to these pray let him call ME to his Character.

SIR PETER. Then I believe we need add no more---if He knows himself He will consider it as the most perfect Punishment that He is known to the world---

CHARLES. If they talk this way to Honesty---what will they say to ME by and bye!

SIR OLIVER. As for that Prodigal---his Brother there------

CHARLES. Aye now comes my Turn---the damn'd Family Pictures will ruin me---

SURFACE. Sir Oliver---Unkle---will you honour me with a hearing---

CHARLES. I wish Joseph now would make one of his long speeches and I might recollect myself a little---

SIR OLIVER. And I suppose you would undertake to vindicate yourself entirely---

SURFACE. I trust I could---

SIR OLIVER. Nay---if you desert your Roguery in its Distress and try to be justified---you have even less principle than I thought you had.---[To CHARLES SURFACE] Well, Sir---and YOU could JUSTIFY yourself too I suppose---

CHARLES. Not that I know of, Sir Oliver.

SIR OLIVER. What[!] little Premium has been let too much into the secret I presume.

CHARLES. True---Sir---but they were Family Secrets, and should not be mentioned again you know.

ROWLEY. Come Sir Oliver I know you cannot speak of Charles's Follies with anger.

SIR OLIVER. Odd's heart no more I can---nor with gravity either---Sir Peter do you know the Rogue bargain'd with me for all his Ancestors---sold me judges and Generals by the Foot, and Maiden Aunts as cheap as broken China!

CHARLES. To be sure, Sir Oliver, I did make a little free with the Family Canvas that's the truth on't:---my Ancestors may certainly rise in judgment against me there's no denying it---but believe me sincere when I tell you, and upon my soul I would not say so if I was not---that if I do not appear mortified at the exposure of my Follies, it is because I feel at this moment the warmest satisfaction in seeing you, my liberal benefactor.

SIR OLIVER. Charles---I believe you---give me your hand again: the ill-looking little fellow over the Couch has made your Peace.

CHARLES. Then Sir---my Gratitude to the original is still encreased.

LADY TEAZLE. [Advancing.] Yet I believe, Sir Oliver, here is one whom Charles is still more anxious to be reconciled to.

SIR OLIVER. O I have heard of his Attachment there---and, with the young Lady's Pardon if I construe right that Blush------

SIR PETER. Well---Child---speak your sentiments---you know---we are going to be reconciled to Charles---

MARIA. Sir---I have little to say---but that I shall rejoice to hear that He is happy---For me---whatever claim I had to his Affection---I willing resign to one who has a better title.

CHARLES. How Maria!

SIR PETER. Heyday---what's the mystery now? while he appeared an incorrigible Rake, you would give your hand to no one else and now that He's likely to reform I'll warrant You won't have him!

MARIA. His own Heart---and Lady Sneerwell know the cause.

[CHARLES.] Lady Sneerwell!

SURFACE. Brother it is with great concern---I am obliged to speak on this Point, but my Regard to justice obliges me---and Lady Sneerwell's injuries can no longer---be concealed---[Goes to the Door.]

Enter LADY SNEERWELL

SIR PETER. Soh! another French milliner egad! He has one in every Room in the House I suppose---

LADY SNEERWELL. Ungrateful Charles! Well may you be surprised and feel for the indelicate situation which your Perfidy has forced me into.

CHARLES. Pray Unkle, is this another Plot of yours? for as I have Life I don't understand it.

SURFACE. I believe Sir there is but the evidence of one Person more necessary to make it extremely clear.

SIR PETER. And that Person---I imagine, is Mr. Snake---Rowley---you were perfectly right to bring him with us---and pray let him appear.

ROWLEY. Walk in, Mr. Snake---

Enter SNAKE

I thought his Testimony might be wanted---however it happens unluckily that He comes to confront Lady Sneerwell and not to support her---

LADY SNEERWELL. A Villain!---Treacherous to me at last! Speak, Fellow, have you too conspired against me?

SNAKE. I beg your Ladyship---ten thousand Pardons---you paid me extremely Liberally for the Lie in question---but I unfortunately have been offer'd double to speak the Truth.

LADY SNEERWELL. The Torments of Shame and Disappointment on you all!

LADY TEAZLE. Hold---Lady Sneerwell---before you go let me thank you for the trouble you and that Gentleman have taken in writing Letters from me to Charles and answering them yourself---and let me also request you to make my Respects to the Scandalous College---of which you are President---and inform them that Lady Teazle, Licentiate, begs leave to return the diploma they granted her---as she leaves of[f] Practice and kills Characters no longer.

LADY SNEERWELL. Provoking---insolent!---may your Husband live these fifty years!

[Exit.]

SIR PETER. Oons what a Fury------

LADY TEAZLE. A malicious Creature indeed!

SIR PETER. Hey---not for her last wish?---

LADY TEAZLE. O No---

SIR OLIVER. Well Sir, and what have you to say now?

SURFACE. Sir, I am so confounded, to find that Lady Sneerwell could be guilty of suborning Mr. Snake in this manner to impose on us all that I know not what to say------however, lest her Revengeful Spirit should prompt her to injure my Brother I had certainly better follow her directly.

[Exit.]

SIR PETER. Moral to the last drop!

SIR OLIVER. Aye and marry her Joseph if you can.---Oil and Vinegar egad:---you'll do very well together.

ROWLEY. I believe we have no more occasion for Mr. Snake at Present---

SNAKE. Before I go---I beg Pardon once for all for whatever uneasiness I have been the humble instrument of causing to the Parties present.

SIR PETER. Well---well you have made atonement by a good Deed at last---

SNAKE. But I must Request of the Company that it shall never be known---

SIR PETER. Hey!---what the Plague---are you ashamed of having done a right thing once in your life?

SNAKE. Ah: Sir---consider I live by the Badness of my Character!---I have nothing but my Infamy to depend on!---and, if it were once known that I had been betray'd into an honest Action, I should lose every Friend I have in the world.

SIR OLIVER. Well---well we'll not traduce you by saying anything to your Praise never fear.

[Exit SNAKE.]

SIR PETER. There's a precious Rogue---Yet that fellow is a Writer and a Critic.

LADY TEAZLE. See[,] Sir Oliver[,] there needs no persuasion now to reconcile your Nephew and Maria---

SIR OLIVER. Aye---aye---that's as it should be and egad we'll have the wedding to-morrow morning---

CHARLES. Thank you, dear Unkle!

SIR PETER. What! you rogue don't you ask the Girl's consent first---

CHARLES. Oh, I have done that a long time---above a minute ago---and She has look'd yes---

MARIA. For Shame---Charles---I protest Sir Peter, there has not been a word------

SIR OLIVER. Well then the fewer the Better---may your love for each other never know---abatement.

SIR PETER. And may you live as happily together as Lady Teazle and I---intend to do---

CHARLES. Rowley my old Friend---I am sure you congratulate me and I suspect too that I owe you much.

SIR OLIVER. You do, indeed, Charles---

ROWLEY. If my Efforts to serve you had not succeeded you would have been in my debt for the attempt---but deserve to be happy---and you over-repay me.

SIR PETER. Aye honest Rowley always said you would reform.

CHARLES. Why as to reforming Sir Peter I'll make no promises---and that I take to be a proof that I intend to set about it---But here shall be my Monitor---my gentle Guide.---ah! can I leave the Virtuous path those Eyes illumine?

Tho' thou, dear Maid, should'st wave [waive] thy Beauty's Sway,
    ---Thou still must Rule---because I will obey:
    An humbled fugitive from Folly View,
    No sanctuary near but Love and YOU:
    You can indeed each anxious Fear remove,
    For even Scandal dies if you approve. [To the audience.]

    EPILOGUE

81

BY MR. COLMAN

I, who was late so volatile and gay,
Like a trade-wind must now blow all one way,
Bend all my cares, my studies, and my vows,
To one dull rusty weathercock---my spouse!
So wills our virtuous bard---the motley Bayes
Of crying epilogues and laughing plays!
Old bachelors, who marry smart young wives,
Learn from our play to regulate your lives:
Each bring his dear to town, all faults upon her---
London will prove the very source of honour.
Plunged fairly in, like a cold bath it serves,
When principles relax, to brace the nerves:
Such is my case; and yet I must deplore
That the gay dream of dissipation's o'er.
And say, ye fair! was ever lively wife,
Born with a genius for the highest life,
Like me untimely blasted in her bloom,
Like me condemn'd to such a dismal doom?
Save money---when I just knew how to waste it!
Leave London---just as I began to taste it!
  Must I then watch the early crowing cock,
The melancholy ticking of a clock;
In a lone rustic hall for ever pounded,
With dogs, cats, rats, and squalling brats surrounded?
With humble curate can I now retire,
(While good Sir Peter boozes with the squire,)
And at backgammon mortify my soul,
That pants for loo, or flutters at a vole?
Seven's the main! Dear sound that must expire,
Lost at hot cockles round a Christmas fire;
The transient hour of fashion too soon spent,
Farewell the tranquil mind, farewell content!
Farewell the plumed head, the cushion'd tete,
That takes the cushion from its proper seat!
That spirit-stirring drum!---card drums I mean,
Spadille---odd trick---pam---basto---king and queen!
And you, ye knockers, that, with brazen throat,
The welcome visitors' approach denote;
Farewell all quality of high renown,
Pride, pomp, and circumstance of glorious town!
Farewell! your revels I partake no more,
And Lady Teazle's occupation's o'er!
All this I told our bard; he smiled, and said 'twas clear,
I ought to play deep tragedy next year.
Meanwhile he drew wise morals from his play,

And in these solemn periods stalk'd away:---
"Bless'd were the fair like you; her faults who stopp'd,
And closed her follies when the curtain dropp'd!
No more in vice or error to engage,
Or play the fool at large on life's great stage."

END OF PLAY

FOOTNTES:

1 ([return](#))
[This PORTRAIT and Garrick's PROLOGUE are not included in Fraser Rae's text.]

2 ([return](#))
[From Sheridan's manuscript.]

3 ([return](#))
[The story in Act I. Scene I., told by Crabtree about Miss Letitia Piper, is repeated here, the speaker being Sir Peter:

SIR PETER. O nine out of ten malicious inventions are founded on some ridiculous misrepresentation---Mrs. Candour you remember how poor Miss Shepherd lost her Lover and her Character one Summer at Tunbridge.

MRS. C. To be sure that was a very ridiculous affair.

CRABTREE. Pray tell us Sir Peter how it was.

SIR P. Why madam---[The story follows.]

MRS. C. Ha ha strange indeed---

SIR P. Matter of Fact I assure you....

LADY T. As sure as can be---Sir Peter will grow scandalous himself---if you encourage him to tell stories.
(Fraser Rae's footnote---Ed.)]

4 ([return](#))
[The words which follow this title are not inserted in the manuscript of the play. (Fraser Rae's footnote.---Ed.)]

5 ([return](#))
[From this place to Scene ii. Act IV. several sheets are missing. (Fraser Rae's footnote.---Ed.)]

Printed in Great Britain
by Amazon

81776972R00051